Assum

A.  ∪eknon

Text copyright © A. A. Sekhon 2018
Design copyright © Billie Hastie 2018
All rights reserved.

A. A. Sekhon has asserted their right under the Copyright, Designs and Patents Act 1988 to be identified as the author of this work.

No part of this book may be reprinted or reproduced or utilised in any form or by electronic, mechanical or any other means, now known or hereafter invented, including photocopying or recording, or in any information storage or retrieval system, without the permission in writing from the Publisher and Author.

This is a work of fiction. Names, characters, businesses, places, events and incidents are either the products of the author's imagination or used in a fictitious manner. Any resemblance to actual persons, living or dead, or actual events is purely coincidental.

This title is intended for the enjoyment of adults, and is not recommended for children due to the mature subject matter it contains.

First published 2018

This edition published 2026
by Rowanvale Books Ltd
The Gate
Keppoch Street
Roath
Cardiff
CF24 3JW
www.rowanvalebooks.com

A CIP catalogue record for this book is available from the British Library.
ISBN: 978-1-83584-112-9

Printed and bound in Great Britain by Bell and Bain Ltd, Glasgow

Dedicated to all who struggle with accepting who they are, or who face oppression because of it. Know that you are not alone.

And to Max, the love of my life.

CHAPTER ONE

He awoke in a morgue in London. It was dark, the middle of a black and blustery March night, the wind rushing and the rain falling hard and cold on the pavement, slicking the cobblestones and forming little traceries of ice where it froze on the fallen leaves thick in the gutters. Yet inside, all was deathly still. The morticians had long since gone home, the lights had been put out, and the only sound to be heard was the creaking of the old building as it stood against the assault of the whirling wind.

God, where am I? he thought in a panic, disoriented and alone in the dark.

He sat up suddenly, a rough cotton sheet sliding off his chest as he did so and coming to rest in bunchy folds at his waist. He felt the cool prick of the air and realised he was naked. There was a hard surface under him—a slab of stone or metal, perhaps. It felt as chill as he did.

He tried to haul himself off the surface, feeling blindly for the floor, and found himself incredibly stiff and sore. He gingerly manoeuvred himself into a standing position. Yet, even once on his feet, he kept one hand on the edge of the slab, half-leaning, as one would when ill, to brace and balance his unsteady frame. And perhaps he was ill, after a manner of speaking: a sickness of the soul, spread to all the body's members and through all the depths of the mind. He felt lightheaded, weak, and vaguely nauseated.

He had experienced extreme disorientation upon awakening, the kind that runs so deep one wakes up with nary a clue as to *who* one even is, much less where one is, what time it is, and how one came to be there. Now for the most part vertical, steadying himself as best he could, he took a moment to try and collect his thoughts. In so doing, he gradually became aware of the general temper of them: rational, inquisitive, and calm, if somewhat weary. There was uncertainty, but not anger—a ponderous, slightly fearful, general wonderment. He plodded along with his many interrogative thoughts, aware of their tone but not really noticing it at first, as if it were something to be taken for granted. Slowly, however, the dull realisation dawned on him, as his sleepiness subsided. When it at last broke through into his conscious mind, it so startled him that he let out a gasp of surprise and amazement. His thoughts, he found, were...*normal*. He was back to normal.

He wished it were not pitch black, wished he had a light, a mirror, *something*, to confirm that this happy discovery was more than a mere hypothesis. He couldn't be sure he wasn't just dreaming. He ran his hands over his face, his head, his body, felt familiar angles and proper proportions, all specifically, naturally, undeniably his. He checked his pulse—yes, his heart beat. He pinched himself hard and felt the ensuing pain—sweet pain! He was *alive*! Overjoyed and exceedingly curious, he thanked God, prayed this might not yet prove just some insubstantial mind-dream, and counted himself perhaps the luckiest man in all of Heaven and Earth. He had been given another chance!

Stumbling about in the dark, he cautiously felt his way round the room, searching for a way out. His outstretched hands could not save his hip from hitting another slab, however, not three feet from the spot where he'd awakened. The impact jarred him, his foot slipped in some unknown fluid, and he toppled forward onto his knees, impacting the underside of his chin on the hard surface.

Temporarily stunned, he stayed where he had fallen for a few brief seconds. When he scrabbled to hoist himself up, his right hand brushed against something on the slab. It felt like skin—cold, still, clammy skin.

A body. The body of a young woman, by the feel of it. He got up hastily. Taking more care now as he felt his way around the room, he noticed there were other bodies. Lots of them.

One part of his mind told him that this all made sense: He must've simply been taken for dead and mistakenly wound up in the mortuary after the incident in his little room. He must have calculated correctly or at least subconsciously (or by some miracle) figured out the precise amount of cyanide to take and still cheat death. He was lucky to be alive. Another, illogical part, however, gave rise to the sneaking suspicion that he had died and gone to Hell, surrounded by scores of corpses.

He searched for a door, a window, anything besides bodies. Eventually, his fingers ran across some more cotton fabric, much like the cloths covering the remains but with a difference: This was vertical and concealed, not a corpse, but a cornice...and a sill. A window. He stood before a curtained window. With one hand, he gently pulled back the drapery, just enough to look through the panes and into the black night beyond. He noticed a bobby passing below a streetlight, the fire-flicker reflecting off the back of the officer's rounded, rain-slicked helmet.

He hastily drew the draperies back together, enswathing the dank, dingy room in darkness once more. It was an unthinking reaction born of fear and desperation; not so long ago, he'd been a wanted man, a fugitive from the law, struggling unsuccessfully to escape an engulfing quagmire of his own creation. He was certain they would've hanged him if they had found him then, so grievous were his iniquities.

But now...now...what? What was to become of him? Did he dare go back to his former life? Could such a return even be attempted? There would be a great deal of explaining to do, of that he had no doubt.

But if his hope held true—if he was, indeed, forever free of his precarious condition—then any amount of questioning would be more than worth the trouble. To have his normal life back, to be sound of health again... Could such a dream ever prove possible? He had his doubts; it all seemed a little too good to be true. Yet he felt this was an opportunity he could ill afford to let pass him by.

First things first, however. It would do him no good to be caught inside the morgue, nor noticed whilst attempting to slip out of it. It would arouse too much suspicion and conjure up questions he'd never be able to properly answer. Best to get out of the place as quickly and quietly as possible. To that end, he searched about in the dark for a door, found one within a matter of minutes, listened carefully for the sounds of anyone on the other side, turned the handle slowly and soundlessly, and carefully let himself out into an adjacent room. He treaded cautiously through it, unable to satisfactorily soften the *shup, shup, shup* of his footfall against the shoddy flooring. Luckily, no one was there to take note of the noise.

With only his death-shroud wrapped round his waist, he continued on to yet another room. He tried the door in the far wall. Locked. He'd have to find some other way out. He discovered a window which overlooked a little alleyway, and (what was more) was easily unlatched. Fortunately, he found himself on the ground floor, so it took him only a short thrust and a jump to get over the windowsill and out of the building.

Landing proved trickier: The lower surface was slick and hard, and he nearly fell flat on his face, losing hold of his hip-blanket in the process. Feeling a bit old and unwieldy for such shenanigans, he steadied himself, then bent down, picked up his linen piece, and hurriedly rewrapped himself. Hunched from cold and fear, he took stock of his surroundings, keeping a sharp eye out for any potential witnesses. The frigid rain had tapered off, thankfully, and was now just a light, spitting drizzle. It flecked his shoulders and clung in little droplets to his hair (brown, greying at the temples). Why, it was hardly more than a good, heavy fog.

Barefoot, freezing, and half-naked, he hurried on miserably, dashing through misty, deserted streets and glowering lamplight, everything around him a fine silhouette. His feet carried him farther and farther away from that cold and lifeless house of corpses, the scenery swirling by him in an almost undifferentiated mist as he traversed lonely quarters and deathly-still squares. The entire city, it seemed, was asleep. He saw no lights in any of the houses or other buildings. The only illumination came from the gas lights along the more well-known and (in the daytime) highly trafficked avenues and boulevards. The little side streets and alleyways held nothing but cold, damp darkness and the smell of rotting leaves.

Suddenly, upon crossing a corner where an alleyway unexpectedly let out into a street bright with gas light, he literally ran into a passerby, the hearty *thwack* of the collision echoing briefly off the rain-soaked bricks of the bystreet's buildings. He stumbled but shortly regained his balance. The newcomer, however, was knocked soundly to the ground by the impact.

'Terribly sorry,' he said automatically, momentarily forgetting his miserable condition and strange accoutrement as his well-bred sense of social decorum kicked in. He had a genuine concern for the wayfarer and her well-being. 'Are you alright, miss?' he asked, extending his hand to help her up.

The girl—perhaps nine or ten years old at most—was dressed in the plain, drab clothes of the lower classes. Her dowdy dress and dingy bonnet served only to make her rain-matted, straw-blonde hair all the brighter by comparison. She got up on her own, then quickly backed away from the stranger, her wary, cocoa-brown eyes never once letting him out of their gaze.

His kelly-green eyes, in contrast, glanced rapidly about as he searched for something soothing to say. He hadn't meant to bowl the poor lass over, and didn't want to deepen his failings by frightening her in addition. A disturbing memory swam to consciousness, threatening to distract his attention, but he mastered himself and kept his composure.

'Again, I apologise,' he reiterated, bowing stiffly at the child. 'I did not realise anyone would be in the process of traversing that corner. I've seen hardly a soul this entire wretched night,' he explained, hoping to clear up any misunderstanding of his intent.

'Then what are you doin' out 'ere, sir, when there's not a soul to be seen? And what 'appened to your clothes?' she enquired in a thick cockney accent, fear turning to suspicion mixed with a mote of curiosity. 'You from Bedlam or somethin'?'

'Bedlam?' he echoed, the unexpectedness of this suggestion catching him off guard. 'No, I—' He laughed. 'I can assure you, I haven't come from an asylum, though I'm certain my current accoutrement must cause me to appear quite queer.'

The gentleness of his gaze seemed oddly familiar to the child, as did his courtesy. Her curiosity, at first a mere candle, now kindled into a brightly blazing bonfire that gradually burned away her fear and mistrust.

'So, what 'appened to you then, sir?' she queried, glancing at the sheet and then back to his face.

'A set of rather extraordinary circumstances,' he replied, though even as he uttered the words, he knew he could never tell her the truth of what had transpired. He doubted she'd believe him even if he spelled the whole sorry affair out for her. And—worse yet—if she did, it could very well lead to trouble with the law again. So, instead, he sold her a vague but believable fib: 'I was robbed on my way to the train station. Two tremendous louts laid hold of me; I am ashamed to say I found myself ineffective in my attempts to overpower them and break free.' His eyes narrowed and his lips tightened as he continued, 'The sneaky blackguards ambushed me from behind; I was caught completely by surprise. They knocked me over the head and took everything. I awoke in an unfamiliar alleyway, with even the clothes on my back gone missing. I was lucky enough to find this linen'—here he gestured toward the meagre cloth he wore—'in a rubbish bin nearby.'

'Seems that's all the luck you've 'ad, mister,' replied the girl in astonishment. There was also a hint of anger in her voice, as if to condemn the abominable actions of the absent (and, unbeknownst to her, imaginary) criminals. Presumably recalling that he'd supposedly been headed for the train station originally, she asked, 'You from outta town, then, or was you just 'eaded out?'

'I...I'm not from around here, actually,' he said with a hint of hesitation, letting the barest wisp of a lowland Scottish accent creep into his otherwise impeccable, upper-class English. In the most limited and literal sense, his statement was true: He really wasn't from this particular quarter of London. No, he had lived in a fine old house on a square in a better part of the city...

Changing the subject, he asked if they might hold their discussion in a more sheltered space or, if she preferred, continue on their separate ways. To the latter, she scoffed, 'Nonsense! A poor gent comes to town, gets beaten and robbed of everythin' 'e 'as, winds up wanderin' the streets on one of the chillest nights of the season in little more than what the good Lord gave 'im, and I'm to just stand 'ere and do nothin' about it?' She shook her head. 'It ain't right,' she asserted, looking him straight in the eye. Nodding a bit to herself, she righteously continued, 'And I won't stand for it. Now come on,' she commanded, gesturing for him to follow. 'You're stayin' the night with Grammy and me.' She began walking purposefully in the direction from which she had first arrived.

He stood still, making no such move to do so. Her offer had taken him by surprise, and he wrestled with himself over what to do now. He had fled from the morgue in a flurry, his mind just short of panic, trying to put as much space as he could between himself and that hideous place in the shortest span of time possible. He came to realise that he had headed for his house automatically, out of habit, without really having been consciously aware of it. Now, however, he paused to ponder: What course of action would prove prudent? Which were the wisest options? He could continue on to his home, but he'd have to concoct some fairly crafty excuses if he wished to leave behind this well-meaning little girl. Furthermore, though he hoped for the best, he had no guarantee that his old life would still be available to him upon his return. If circumstances took a turn for the worse, he'd wind up right back in the same mess he had so lately (and miraculously) managed to circumvent.

He supposed there was no harm in following her home. His previous ordeal had sapped much of his spiritual strength, and his recent run from the morgue, while accomplishing his aim of escape, had otherwise served only to steal away the last of his physical reserves. Bordering on the brink of absolute exhaustion, he felt stiff, sore, frigid, and more than a little woozy. He found he had to squat down, palms reluctantly resting on the ice-cold cobblestones for support, to allow a sufficient amount of blood to reach his brain to keep him conscious.

The child, hitherto walking ahead, turned around when there was a distinct lack of footfall following her. Seeing the stranger looking so sickly, she swiftly made her way over the slick paving-stones and stood at his side.

'Blimey, are you alright, sir?' she asked, her eyebrows raised in concern.

He breathed heavily a few times, then reassured her, ''Tis nothing. For a moment, I feared I might faint, but I feel nearly fine now.' He looked up at her.

'I'm surprised you 'aven't caught your death of cold out 'ere tonight,' opined the youngster.

She held out her hand to hoist him up. Even after he rose, she helped support his feeble frame, allowing him to lean on her a bit. He was slightly feverish, and he knew it. He suspected she detected it as well, though she could not know the circumstances behind the original inducement of this state in him.

How long was it since he had first felt so sick? How long—previous to his death-still, poison-induced slumber—since he'd been able to sleep the least bit soundly? He had been through a kind of mental anguish, a thousand tiny, tortuous deaths... He almost wondered how he'd managed to carry on at all, what with everything he had endured. But the human animal could be an awfully stubborn creature, clinging to life with an undreamed-of tenacity, its every faculty tuned toward survival. Adaptability, creativity, smarts—Man had them all. He could even take calculated risks...especially when educated.

Thus was this well-schooled, cyanide-swallowing stranger able to be there alive at all, sickly though he was, supported by a kindly, smallish child, strolling down the rain-soaked streets of London.

***

It was in the wee hours of this black, late-winter morning that they arrived at their destination, someplace at the end of the world—or, at least, a very different part of London than a man of his breeding had any proper business being in. It was obviously a working-class neighbourhood, though not nearly as bad as certain streets in Soho or the unsavoury sections of the city's East End.

She led him into the house—little more than a hovel, really—and they shortly entered the Lilliputian living room. There they encountered an elderly woman sitting on an ancient rocker by the fireside. The meagre flames produced a pale, orange glow that flickered irregularly over her wrinkled, timeworn features. A black mourner's cap, complete with pulled-back veil, covered most of her wispy, greying hair. There was an air of resigned sadness to this widow, as if she kept on living by simple force of habit alone. And, to the stranger, there was something disturbingly familiar about her as well, though he couldn't discern exactly what or why.

The girl's announcement—'Grammy, we got a visitor tonight'—proffered a happy distraction from this strange suspicion, but only briefly. As the crone arose from her chair (more quickly than he would've expected), he caught a glimpse of her profile, silhouetted against the fire for one split second. Though there was nothing overtly unusual about it, the image struck something deep within him, something submerged and buried that he could not quite identify. For no known reason, it sent a series of chills straight down his spine and set his teeth a-chattering.

The waif-girl, thinking he was just cold, sought to usher him closer to the fire.

The lines on the old woman's face bespoke adamance, but not mean-spiritedness. As she beheld this strange new visitor, however, her eyes widened in surprised alarm and then quickly narrowed as she raised her guard.

'What've you gone and done now, Ginny?' she more scolded than asked the youngster, in an odd accent somewhere between cockney and middle-class. 'Haven't I warned you against bringin' in folk off the street? We ain't the local poorhouse, missy.'

'Terribly sorry for the intrusion, madam,' he managed, though inwardly he was feeling sicker by the minute. The sound of the senior's voice hadn't helped him any. There was something in it that had grated on his nerves, twisting up his innards for no perceptible reason, and he began to grow simultaneously weak and on edge.

The child's voice afforded him a slight reprieve. He tried his best to focus on only it, in an urgent effort to still his all-too-feverish mind and body. He concentrated on its cadence, on the lilt it took on at certain times, on her coarse but honest manner of phrasing things, as she began to tell her grandmum all about this poor chap's (presumable) misadventures. It was enough to temporarily soothe his spirit, and his mind quieted a little. Then it faded into blackness as the stress of standing there at last took its toll on his tired, overtaxed body. His previous lack of sound sleep, the exhausting exertions of this night's flight, and the inescapable, fog-damp chill all finally proved too much. They combined and caught up with his fever-weakened constitution, and he fainted.

CHAPTER TWO

He awoke beneath an unfamiliar ceiling. It was plain and low and of no fine craftsmanship. He stared at it, unable to place where he was, unsure even of who he was...for a moment.

'Feelin' any better?' came a voice from somewhere above him and off to the side.

He turned his head, discovering in the process that it rested on a flat, cold, chillingly familiar surface. He realised he was recumbent and covered with what felt like a sheet of some kind. He wondered for an instant if he were not back in the mortuary, waking up to relive the miserable night all over again, *ad infinitum*, as some type of purgatorial punishment.

His fears were unfounded, however. He soon glimpsed the gracious girl who had had pity on him and taken him in. She was sitting a few feet away from where he lay on the house's chill floorboards. A blanket—a nice, knitted, *dry* one—covered him over, no doubt provided by the caring child. Though it did little to combat the icy cold seeping into his skin from the floor, it was better than nothing, and protected his modesty, at least. He appreciated the gesture.

'A bit,' returned the sickly looking chap as he slowly sat up, his mind putting together what had happened. 'Have I fainted?'

'Aye, that you did, sir,' the youngster replied. 'Fainted dead away, you did. Gave Grammy and me quite the scare. Though she finally took pity on you on account of it.'

He regarded her quizzically, cocking a brow and tilting his head a fraction of an inch.

'Whatever do you mean?' he queried.

'Well, it's only 'cause you're dire ill that she's lettin' you stay at all. You see, sir,'—here she glanced at a closed door to her right and his left and lowered her voice—'me grandmum ain't exactly the world's most 'ospitable sort. She wasn't always that way, of course. In fact, while Granpoppy—God rest 'is soul—was still alive, she could be downright charitable. But ever since 'e passed, she ain't been the same. She worries about money, and about strangers and other folk doin' us wrong. I think maybe someone did Granpoppy wrong, but I was too little to remember anythin', and Grammy never talks about it. Alls I know is, we 'ad to move 'ere right after, and that's when Grammy started actin' such. She 'ardly lets outside folks into the 'ouse nowadays—'cept for the landlord and the parson, of course. And she's always goin' on about 'ow we're goin' to be put out on the street if we can't sell enough stuff to people to pay up the rent.' She stopped, as if just remembering something. Her brows drew up and knitted together, and she clapped both hands over her lips as she realised what she had done. 'Blast!' she cried, startling the stranger.

'What?' he asked quickly, disturbed to see her thus distraught. 'Whatever is the matter, child?'

'I forgot,' she said, worry and regret patent in her tone, 'I plumb forgot, Grammy told me not to speak of the family troubles to no one else! She's always sayin' 'ow we can't afford to make our name any worse than it is already.'

'Worse than it is already?' echoed her ailing guest. It surprised him that a person in such undesirable socioeconomic straits would care very much about her name or reputation.

'I don't know what 'appened, really,' explained the girl. 'But some of the blokes 'round 'ere is always callin' me nasty names, and sayin' unkind things about me granpop—God grant 'im peace.' She paused, then chided herself, 'But there I go, goin' off again! I oughtn't to, I know. But some of the things they say are just so—so 'urtful, mister!'

'How positively abominable!' he exclaimed, his brow lowering and his lips forming a firm line. 'They've no right to say anything ill of you, absolutely no right!' For, to his mind, she was the very picture of humble Christian charity. He had no doubt she could do no less than turn the other cheek to these affronts.

'Well, I pop 'em good, sometimes, if it's one of the smaller boys what's sayin' it,' she declared a touch proudly.

So much for the perfect innocence of children, he reflected. He recalled also how certain lads he'd grown up with could be rather less than kind. It was his own mistake, he supposed, for thinking children of the fairer sex were somehow sweeter, naturally more delicate, and less inclined to violence. Perhaps, in the end, they were simply brought up differently. No one was immune. And as he thought about it, he realised that children prefigured adults, did they not? And what adult was completely free from sin or flaws of character? Oftentimes, the young could be much crueller than their elders (who, if nothing else, had learned to mask their desires with a certain degree of decorum). Though he had tried to steer clear of such base mischief in his own childhood, aiming to be neither a perpetrator nor a victim, he had seen it happen to others. Though a large man now, he had been runty and bookish as a boy. He knew he would've suffered numerous indignities at the hands of his peers had it not been for his name and the weight it carried. *Ah, it all comes back to that, doesn't it? One's name. One's background. One's reputation and standing in bloody social circles, never mind what sort of person one actually* is—*kind or cruel, giving or miserly, wholesome or perverse...*

Perverse. His mind lingered unintentionally on that last word. It drew up images that threatened to divert his stream of thought in new and undesirable directions.

He couldn't afford that right now. Instead, he turned his attention back to the girl and her unfortunate social predicament. He wondered if it were not possible to bring his own resources to bear and, perhaps, restore her family's good name. Musing thusly, he suddenly realised that he didn't even know what that name *was*.

'Sorry to change the subject,' he stated, 'but it occurs to me that I am a guest in your home and yet do not even know your name.'

'Oh, bless me, I clean forgot!' she exclaimed, chastising herself for her lack of manners.

'Quite understandable, given the circumstances,' he soothed in kindly tones.

'Still, I feel I oughta 'ave done it proper,' she apologised. 'Grammy's always sayin' so, anyways.' With that, she stood and backed up a bit. Performing a quick curtsy, she said, with as much grace as she could summon, 'Virginia Flowers. A pleasure to meet you.' She tried to remain serious as she rose, but couldn't completely suppress an impish grin which broke through at the last moment. 'You can call me "Ginny" if you want,' she informed him, back to her usual demeanour now. 'Most folks does.'

'It is, as you say, a pleasure,' he returned, attempting stiffly to get up from the floor, quilt strategically situated.

'Oh, blimey, don't bother gettin' up, sir,' voiced the greatly surprised young girl. 'I was only practisin', and you're 'alf sick!'

'I feel significantly better than I did previously,' he reassured her, rising to a reasonably stable (if still a smidge sickly looking) standing position. Going through the proper motions, he introduced himself. 'Harry Edwards,' said he, giving her a name that was removed enough from his own that she'd never be able to trace his true identity if things didn't work out, but close enough to the truth that he could explain the discrepancy away as a misunderstanding on her part if they did. 'And I can assure you, I've no problem with civilities. In fact,' he observed, 'I am rather enjoying these right now, and find it, I daresay, delightful to act in so proper a fashion. It contributes mightily to my feeling human again after my recent travails.' In this, he spoke the truth. It was nice, actually, for a change. Downright pleasurable, even. It had been some months since he'd been able to trust himself enough to interact with anyone in a formal social setting with any degree of reliability. *Curious*, he remarked inwardly, *that I should have come to miss it so.* He had once sought to escape the very social circles wherein these rituals were required, had hated the bonds of obligation they signified and reinforced. Now he found these civil customs strangely comforting.

'So your name's 'arry, then, is it?' Ginny queried. Not waiting on an answer, she averred, 'That was me granpoppy's name: 'arold Denman, may 'e rest in peace.' She beamed and gave a short, excited sigh upon suddenly realising *that* was whom he reminded her of. 'So is your name 'arold, too, sir?' she asked, curious.

'Henry, actually,' he rejoined, but it was patent from his expression that his mind was elsewhere. 'Was your grandfather a doctor?' he enquired abruptly, then added, for politeness' sake, 'If you don't mind my asking.'

'No, I—I don't mind none, Mister Edwards, not at all,' she replied, surprised by his query. 'Aye, 'e was a doctor, sir—a surgeon, if I'm not wrong.' She cocked her head at him, her interest piqued. "Ow did you know that?'

He paused to consider how much he should tell her.

'I am myself trained in the medical profession,' he explained. 'Doctor Denman was well known and very well respected in certain circles. His research was the talk of the most skilled physicians, his success in assuring his students' comprehension of the subject quite commendable, and his own surgical expertise entirely enviable.' He halted briefly, beholding the young girl, and added, 'Though all this was, of course, before your time. It's been decades since last he lectured.'

'Blimey. I never knew,' she uttered softly, taking in the revelation. 'I 'ad no idea Granpoppy was so great a surgeon.' She realised something. 'And you said you're a doctor, too?' she asked.

'Among other things.' He nodded.

'Well, I suppose I oughta call you "*Doc* Edwards", then, oughtn't I?' she said with a smile. 'You're plumb full of surprises, you are.'

He chuckled at her statement and her pairing of title and name. He was glad he could laugh about it, even if only ironically—glad the nightmare was, at last, finally over. It seemed so, anyway. He had thus far encountered no evidence to indicate the contrary, no sign that spelled out an impending doom. He felt relieved—playful, even—as if he had tossed aside his troubles like so much rubbish.

'You know, I had great professional respect for Harold Denman,' he informed her, speaking the truth while at the same time nimbly moving the conversation away from himself. 'It is an honour to make the acquaintance of his granddaughter, even under such unusual circumstances as these.' Something occurred to him. 'I take it, then, your grandmother is his widow?'

'That I am,' came a voice to his left, as the door to the dwelling's modest bedroom swung wide. Emerging through the portal, the old woman continued, 'Though what business that is of yours, I can hardly say.' She looked at him as he stood there clad in only the blanket she'd provided him. 'Seems you're feelin' better,' she observed. 'Better enough to stand there makin' idle chit-chat with a nine-year-old about things what don't concern you.'

'I'll be ten come April, Grammy,' the girl grumbled, a bit put out at being referred to thusly.

'Don't you go mouthin' off to me, young missy,' countered the widow, not about to have any of it. 'You've stretched my patience thin enough as it is.' Here she glanced at the doctor while adding further, 'If I was you, I wouldn't test my luck.' Though her last statement was ostensibly meant for Ginny, it was clearly directed at him, too.

'I am duly honoured to make your acquaintance,' said the gentleman in response to all this, opting for civility to try and smooth the old bird's ruffled feathers. 'As I was just telling your granddaughter here, I had the utmost professional respect for your late husband, and in fact attended more than a few of his medical lectures.'

The harsh lines around the crone's eyes softened almost imperceptibly. Though she was obviously still not keen on having a stranger in her house, nor favourably predisposed towards him, she would at least allow him to continue speaking.

'I am terribly sorry to have imposed thusly,' he proceeded, 'and you have shown such a wealth of spirit in allowing me to stay here in my hour of need—Ginny can tell you how I was ambushed near the railway station—that I'm afraid it may prove impossible to ever repay you fully. However,' and here he looked her directly in the eye, 'I should sincerely like to try.'

The old woman regarded him silently, her face an unintelligible mask. He was most unsure what she might be thinking. Though he normally prided himself on his ability to read people, the only impression he could wring from her look was one of impenetrability. Had his plea been well received? Or would the widow cast him—in his current, half-indecent (dis)array—out onto the street without further ado, ruining the chance for a better life for herself and her granddaughter in one swift stroke?

This pregnant, silent moment ticked uncomfortably on and on.

Finally, her craggy features softened, and she briefly lowered her eyes. He knew, in that instant, that she had found him genuine. His words had touched something deep within her, a feeling long ago shut down, forgotten, atrophying over years of neglect. Now, however, as she once more met his gaze, he *knew*, through all his self-divided soul, that it had been revivified. What he saw shining, ever so tremulously, from her eyes...was *trust*.

***

In the ensuing conversation, the wizened dam revealed (in an unexpectedly civil manner) the following information of import: Margaret Pippin (the old woman's maiden name) had married the good Dr Denman nearly four decades ago. ('Would've been our fortieth anniversary, come mid-April,' as Madge put it.) She had been beautiful then, and not just in the physical sense. She'd had real spark, a certain feistiness or vibrant spirit. Even now, that fire was not yet fully extinguished, tempered though it was by a hard life and higher-than-healthful helping of heartache and life's bitterness. Harold Denman's background had been decidedly upper-crust—not quite nobility, but still very successful, respected, and respectable. He had found Madge ever so much more interesting than those high-society damsels who'd been bred to be either passively haughty or dreadfully dull. Madge Pippin, by contrast, had come from a lower-middle-class family of shop-owning tailors and seamstresses.

Thus Dr Denman's genuine affection for Miss Pippin—and, what was more important, his earnest desire to actually make her his *wife*—had come as quite a shock to his poor parents. Such things simply were not done, after all. But Harold had been adamant. And as the elder Denmans' only son, it had been him on whom they had to rely in their old age. (Truth be told, his doting mother had helped convince Harold's father, concerned as she was with her son's happiness above all else.) Thus, they'd allowed Harold certain excesses, his marriage to Madge being one of these. He had been, after all, a good-natured and otherwise respectable fellow. He'd cared deeply for his family and their well-being, not to mention his devotion to the furtherance of knowledge and the healing of the sick. He'd always given back to the community: Free of charge, he'd treated those too poor to afford a physician, and encouraged his students to do likewise. Therefore, a marriage to someone of the middle classes hadn't been unforgiveable, all things considered. His parents had allowed him this inscrutable indulgence and put it down to love or eccentricity.

For her part, Madge had never dreamed that the good doctor would go so far as to give her a marriage proposal, and had been only too happy to accept (as had her parents). She'd loved Harold dearly, loved his subtle wit and his magnanimity, his giving spirit and imperturbable disposition. Most of all, she'd loved that he'd treated her as an actual, *thinking* human being, with a will and mind all her own. Around him, and him only, she'd felt free to reveal her own best self—the loyal, tender, vulnerable lady beneath her customary outer layers of impenetrable toughness and rapid-fire wit.

They'd lived with Harold's parents, Dr Thomas and Mrs Elizabeth Brodie Denman, on Hanover Square. Theirs was a fine old eighteenth-century manor that they had purchased from the Earl of Plymouth. It had a courtyard round the back. Beyond this and slightly to the left lay a smaller, plainer building, made of brick and intended more for function than form. This had been Dr Denman's operating theatre, a very serviceable little edifice, two storeys high, where he'd performed surgeries and dissections, and lectured to his many well-bred students.

This, Madge's current visitor knew already, for he had been one such student, and he told the old widow as much. What he did not let on was that he had, in fact, bought that very property, as well as the adjoining courtyard and the house, not long after Dr Denman's downfall. Thus it was that he knew also of a certain narrow flight of steps leading to a private, upper room—a place he had spent many nights of late—attached to this selfsame surgical structure, even though the widow Denman failed to illuminate this fact for him.

Most of the Denmans—Harold, his parents, and, of course, his wife, Madge— had lived together in the house and on its grounds. Thomas's much younger sister, and Harold's aunt, Claire, however, had not. She had married a Mr Rory Falstaff and, thus, resided with him in a separate house, in another part of town. Claire had actually been closer in age to her nephew, Harold, than to her own brother. Claire and Thomas' mother had married at age sixteen; nearly a year later, she'd given birth to Thomas. Born in August of 1805, Claire had been twenty-six and a half years younger than her sibling. (She had certainly come as a shock to their mother, who'd been a ripe old forty-three at the time.) In May of 1831, when Claire had been nearly twenty-six, she'd married Rory, who'd already turned a solid thirty-one. The couple had had difficulty conceiving, but had finally been blessed with one child: a son, Richard (called 'Dick'), born on the sixth of August, right at the height of the sweltering-hot summer of 1844. Thus, though Richard Falstaff had in truth been Harold Denman's cousin, the twenty-six-year age gap had made theirs a relationship more along the lines of nephew and uncle, and they'd half-jokingly referred to each other as such.

Dick had attended a smattering of his 'uncle' Harold's lectures when the former was in his early twenties and the latter his late forties. And indeed, Madge's visitor could vouch for this, for he had been in audience at some of these very demonstrations, even into his thirties, for he was always open to expanding his base of knowledge and learning new medical techniques.

Though he and Dick Falstaff had never been formally introduced, Henry realised after Madge's description that he had *seen* Dr Denman's dark-haired 'nephew' there and had been struck by the aura of arrogance emanating out the young Master Falstaff. To Henry, Dick had looked as if he'd thought he had the world by the tail and it owed him a living, to boot. Henry had been singularly unimpressed. The appellation 'supercilious little pig's pizzle' had come to mind. But he had said nothing. After all, he'd had no quarrel with the man and felt it wasn't his place to judge, really. Though, at the time, Henry had been in only his early thirties, he'd still thought of the decade-younger Dick as a creature different from himself, subject to the whims and follies of youth. An over-developed sense of self-importance was, Henry'd reflected, not to be entirely unexpected on the young man's part. Still, he'd had no desire whatsoever to have any truck with the fellow. For, while the morgue-fled doctor had indeed been a bit wild in his own energetic youth, he'd had no wish to intentionally instigate conflict where there was none. Nor had he slandered any man's good name in order to improve his own social standing. In these respects, as it turned out, he differed a great deal from Dick Falstaff.

Dick had wanted his 'uncle' Harold's money (so Madge was convinced), and soon found himself in a position to get it. Rory Falstaff—as well as Claire Denman, incidentally—had died a few years after his son had finished his medical training. Thomas and Elizabeth Denman had long ago passed away, and Harold and Madge's only child, by then sixteen, had been a girl they'd christened Genevieve. As neither Madge nor Genevieve could inherit the bulk of Harold's wealth, Dick had stood to benefit greatly if anything ill befell Dr Denman. (Madge asserted that the surviving Falstaff had also desired to see the well-liked and highly respected doctor take a dive, socially speaking.) Thus, Dick had done everything he could dream of to discredit him. Falstaff had spared no effort. He'd bribed some of the less serious students to stop attending Denman's surgical demonstrations. He'd challenged many of Harold's time-tested methods— under the guise of scholarly debate and the furtherance of learning, of course. He had even bought up a great number of corpses from the purveyors of cadavers. The ensuing shortage of bodies had meant that the great surgeon and anatomist had, for a time, had nothing on which to practise the more visceral aspects of his craft for the benefit of the few remaining eager students (Henry included), who'd thenceforward had nothing visual to learn by.

By far the worst action that Dick had taken, however, had been to start a series of rumours—wicked, vicious, malicious rumours regarding Harold's supposed nighttime activities and purported proclivities. High society had only barely accepted one of its own marrying a middle-class woman. It had brooked no tolerance when that same doctor had found himself rumoured to engage in acts perverse and un-Christian in nature. This unholy combination had been enough to seal the doom of Dr Denman. After these rumours had made the rounds, no one would have anything to do with the man—not even his friends, for they'd feared to have their good names sucked down in the eddy of this damning scandal simply by associating with him.

Rumours are one thing...hard evidence, another. Yet the final mark against Denman had been struck when a dark-haired, young-looking, lower-class man of slight build (no doubt paid off by Falstaff, Madge asserted) had come forward. He'd claimed to be

Harold's lover. Shocked, the good doctor had fervently denied this accusation, but it had made no difference in the end. After all, no man wanted to be examined by a doctor he could not trust. This had been the very last straw and had broken poor Dr Denman. Medicine and Madge had been the two true loves of Harold's life, the only things for which he'd felt real passion. After the scandal, one of these had been denied him forever and, because of this, he'd no longer been able to provide very well for the other. Additionally, it'd become a near impossibility that he'd ever find even a halfway-decent match to marry his daughter.

'That is absolutely appalling!' interjected Henry when the widow Denman related this part of the story. 'I had no idea Dr Falstaff was such an utter cad!'

He felt foolish for having given the fellow the benefit of the doubt, as well as a pang of guilt at not having seen how Dick had manipulated events, to the detriment of Dr Denman. Granted, Henry had not abandoned his mentor completely: He had continued to correspond with him privately and had done everything he could (within the bounds of discretion) to try to restore the elder man's good name. Henry had called in a lawyer—one of his oldest, dearest friends and closest confidant—in an attempt to lessen the blow of the worst strike against Harold: They'd set out to discredit Denman's young 'lover'. After all, they'd reasoned, why should anyone believe the word of an East End rent-boy over that of a theretofore-esteemed pillar of the community? But other witnesses had claimed to have seen the youth and the doctor together at a particular brothel. Henry hadn't believed a word they'd said. These people had been lower-class, all of them—and, in his estimation, easily bribed. Yet neither he nor the attorney had been able to make them alter their stories. Henry had, at the time, surmised that someone (Falstaff, he now realised) had paid these poverty-stricken folk rather heavily, or else threatened them with something unpleasant if they'd changed their tune. In the end, his lawyer friend had given up, saying, 'The damage is done, Henry. There's nothing for it. Let this go before your own name is blackened.' He had reluctantly agreed.

Yet Henry had not just sat by and let Dr Denman go down in flames. It simply hadn't been in him to do such a thing. Though he'd been able to do nothing to save Harold's name, he'd felt that he could, at least, do something to ease the family's financial troubles after the elder physician's business had dried up. He'd known the Denmans would be alright for a while. The family fortune, after all, had been fairly large. This last fact was evidence to him that money had not been Falstaff's main goal. After all, Dick could not have inherited it except in the event of Harold's death, whereas all that had happened immediately had been the blackening of

Denman's name. Madge insisted that, while the name-ruining might have been the first step, it had been only a means to an end. She was certain that all Dick had ever really been after was money. She 'proved' this by citing the fact that Dick had, indeed, finally inherited her late husband's assets when the latter had died in March of 1880, some six years ago, and a full twelve years after the rumours had first begun.

It troubled Henry greatly to hear this. Though he did not reveal it to Madge, he had (knowing Harold's pride would never have allowed him to accept a handout from anyone) bought the family's home, its grounds, and the old operating theatre from Dr Denman for an intentionally exorbitant sum. Henry had had to do some convincing, of course, pointing out that the house was so grand and lovely that it was well worth the price to him. It had, after all, been getting more and more difficult to find fine old houses that hadn't been cut up into flats or decayed along with their neighbourhoods. In the end, Denman had really had no choice but to accept. He'd needed money—not just for himself, but for his wife and their daughter. (Despite Madge's protests that she could more than pull her own weight, Harold hadn't wanted either woman to have to work.) He'd known he'd been lucky, very lucky, to get such a generous offer as Henry's for the house. It had also been likely that the surgical theatre would've gone unsold otherwise, or else been converted into mediocre apartments or a slaughterhouse or some such. Henry'd hoped that, with a doctor buying it—a former student, no less—Harold had at least been able to console himself that it wouldn't go completely unused, so far as its intended purpose was concerned. In the end, Dr Denman had taken the money and moved elsewhere in the city, to someplace more affordable, he and his family living off the sum Henry'd paid for the house et al.

Not knowing where his mentor had relocated, Henry had lost touch with him shortly thereafter. He had at that point never actually met Madge nor Genevieve and, after losing contact with Harold, hadn't dreamt he ever would. And yet, here he was, sitting in the widow Denman's cramped little home, the old woman explaining how Genevieve had married a factory worker by the name of Geoffrey Flowers in April of 1875, how Geoffrey had up and died not eight months later (and with Genevieve five months pregnant, too), how Genevieve had passed away giving birth to little Virginia, and all the (few) joys and (many) sorrows of the intervening years, including Harold's death in 1880. The old woman described how she and Ginny had managed to scrape by, selling matches and flowers, respectively.

Henry sat there, listening to all this, commenting occasionally, but mainly just absorbing what was said. He happened to feel a touch queasy when the widow mentioned that she sold boxes of lights, but he put it down to the shock of learning what she and her granddaughter had now been reduced to.

Madge also explained that her health had deteriorated some as she aged, and that she got sick periodically. Though she usually preferred to tough it out, she occasionally did have to break down and send Ginny to fetch a doctor. This, as it happened, was exactly the reason the young girl had been running down the street this very night, when she bumped into Henry. As it turned out, she had, indeed, brought a doctor back to her grandmum.

Remarkable, observed Henry silently. *Positively remarkable.*

CHAPTER THREE

It was by now very early morning, 'round about half past three or so, and Madge began to slump in her chair with fatigue. Her happenstance houseguest noticed that her cough sounded worse as well. He insisted she go lie down and get some rest—doctor's orders!—though it was clear she'd much rather have stayed up and chatted with him a while longer. But, as her granddaughter's welfare was dependent on her health and as her visitor was a qualified physician, she took heed of his advice and trundled off to her room. She firmly told Ginny that she ought to go to bed as well. Despite the girl's assertions to the contrary, it was patent that she was quite tired, so she, too, soon retired, leaving Henry alone with his thoughts. Having hit his second wind midway through listening to Mrs Denman, he now found his efforts to seek slumber frustratingly futile.

It is no use, he thought, lying back, arms crossed, resigning himself to his condition. He had a kind of nervousness about him, a sort of shaky, wiry energy, and soon sat up, alone in the dark. He could not keep still. It was as if the restlessness of his body reflected the selfsame state of his mind. What was he doing here, after all? He debated what to do next. He thought back on his past, considered his future—his many possible futures—and wondered, now and again, if this were not all just some passing dream.

But he knew it was real, knew that the impossible (or at least *highly* improbable) had happened. He did not doubt that there had to be a reason for it. Providence was a strange master, and his was an unquestionably unusual case altogether, but...

In the end, who can know the mind of God? he thought. *Perhaps free will and fate walk side by side. After all, God is supposed to be all-knowing...* An idea entered in. *I cannot hope to redeem myself by anything I do. Nothing—no works—can ever wipe clean the black iniquities of my past, or set aright the evil I have done. That, I realise. Yet, perhaps by faith...* He found himself praying. *O God, You know my heart is contrite, You more than any soul on this Earth. Please, let this nightmare at last be at an end. Please...*

He wondered, in a part of his mind he wished he could deny, whether all this were not some grand cosmic trick, a deception, a joke for God's benefit, to make him think himself alright, only to later have the pleasant illusion ripped away by Satan himself and find himself in Hell, to be tormented for all eternity for all the wrongs he had committed. He chastised himself immediately after the thought arose—for was it not the height of arrogance to presume God's motives so base and petty?—and, in an almost childlike manner, apologised silently to Him. He fervently wished he could shut out that part of his mind, that such thoughts as these would trouble him no longer. Yet he recognised anew in this desire the slippery slope that had caused him (and many others) so much pain, and which had so nearly culminated in his demise. *No, none of that*, he admonished himself. He was happy for his life as it was, glad to be alive, really, and he was not about to waste the second chance that God or fate had so graciously given him. He was content, perfectly content...

He knew it was a lie the instant he thought it. He knew that he deceived himself. But it didn't matter. Life wasn't always perfect. It was the thought—or, rather, the emotion behind the thought—that counted. And he truly was grateful.

He decided he'd first pay a visit to his old friend, the lawyer. John would, naturally, have many questions, and Henry had every intention of setting the record straight with him (if he hadn't already read the doctor's letter). He wasn't sure precisely what he'd say to his old cohort. He ran several sample scenarios through his head, trying to get a feel for what form the conversation might take, but to no avail. No, there was nothing for it but to talk to the man himself. He also wanted to discuss Madge and Ginny's situation with John, to get his advice and see if anything could be done. Henry vowed to do so first thing in the morning.

This decision made, his mind grew just less active enough to allow him to fall into a state of mild consciousness and half-dreams, undeniably far from sleep, but not exactly awake, either. His thoughts drifted from one thing to another, sometimes brushing by ideas without ever really attaching themselves to them, like slow-swirling clouds around a mountain range's peaks. He continued on in this fitful state until, nearly two hours later, sleep finally found him.

***

Ginny woke him accidentally not a half hour afterward, sometime before dawn.

'My dear girl, whatever are you doing up so early?' queried Henry groggily. He felt as though he hadn't slept at all.

'Oh, bless me, Doctor Edwards!' she exclaimed, then immediately hushed herself. Dropping her voice down to a whisper, she explained, 'Grammy's asleep. I was so busy tryin' not to wake 'er that I plumb forgot you was layin' right there!' She looked apologetic and slightly embarrassed. 'I 'ope I didn't step on you or nothin'.'

'No, no, I am perfectly fine,' he assured her, while inwardly he cursed at the pain throbbing through his left thumb. 'You only grazed me.'

'Oh, good,' Ginny half sighed with relief. She then continued on toward the door, saying, 'I was just on me way out to sell flowers.' Her hand on the doorknob, she paused and turned to the doctor. 'You 'eadin' out, too, today?'

He had been wondering how she proposed to sell flowers when she obviously had none on her and the building, from the look of it, had no garden adjacent. Her question, however, swept these thoughts from his mind. He found himself answering her:

'Why, yes. Of course. You and Mrs Denman have been most kind, yet I cannot, in good conscience, take advantage of your hospitality for any longer than good manners and common sense deem necessary.'

Ginny began to protest, but Henry put up his hand.

'I must insist,' he countered. 'I have imposed upon you and your grandmother for entirely too long and, to tell the truth, must take my leave this very morning.'

With this, he rose, clad in the dark-brown garments Madge Denman had bequeathed him the night before, that he might be presentable for their conversation. These clothes were of a cut that had once been considered dashingly dapper, but was now completely out of fashion. (Their like had not been seen in thirty years.)

'They were Harold's, Doctor Edwards,' the widow had told him. 'He and I would dance the night away, him wearin' that outfit, and I in a fancy dress. Oh, you oughta've seen us, doctor…'

He had refused the suit at first, feeling it improper (and more than a little morbid) to wear the garb of his departed mentor. Madge had been most adamant, however, that such should come to pass. After all, who better than an old and eager student of Harold's, so coincidentally brought into the lives of his widow and granddaughter, a fellow doctor, a perfect gentleman...who better in the world to wear his clothes?

'At least they'll see some use again,' Mrs Denman had remarked. And, truth be told, Henry's initial refusals had been, he knew, half-hearted. It wouldn't have done to sit there half-naked, attempting to carry on a conversation. Besides, he'd known he would need vestments for the morning, when he intended to venture out. Still, he'd felt most odd about accepting Madge's offer.

The clothes fit him almost perfectly, though. They hung a little loosely due to Henry's current state of half-emaciation, but the basic proportions were nearly identical. He had known Dr Denman in Harold's later, more corpulent years, and would never have guessed the man had once been this size, *his* size. It was a tad eerie, all of it. So many chance events, all fitting together, somehow... Henry wondered what all this was leading up to. Was there some greater purpose, good or ill? Or was his mind merely looking for meaning where there was none to be found?

Well, whatever the case, he would endeavour to do his best, of that he was now more than certain. He felt a faint and glowing sense of...well, he wasn't sure exactly what it was. He hadn't experienced such a feeling in quite some time. He could make things right, and he knew it. He was sure he would do it, one way or another.

And so it was with purpose that he set out this morn, after bidding Ginny goodbye and thanking her once more for her kindness. He made his way through dingy, narrow streets, the path winding and the buildings cramped close together. The dead-blue half-light of pre-dawn imbued these surroundings with a strange, flat cast that bordered on pallor, serving more to create shadow than to give any real light. Yet of all this the good doctor seemed wilfully unaware, as if stubbornly refusing to acknowledge the less-than-pleasant aspects of his environment—lest, by getting sidetracked, he let them overwhelm and eventually topple his current, upright frame of mind. No, he would keep a positive, purposeful outlook, paying them no heed. He walked with a solid, confident step through London's version of Purgatory—Purgatory, not Hell. For this neighbourhood's denizens, bad-off as they were, would not be amiss in thanking God each day that they lived here and not scurrilous Soho or, Heaven forbid, the city's East End.

He kept walking until he came upon an old, shabby little park, obviously long-neglected, where something nevertheless caught his eye. At the far end of the park, a small, scrawny girl squirmed through an overgrown hedge. She slipped into the abandoned flowerbed, where some ancient rosebushes had gone wild and taken over the once prim and well-manicured garden. She struggled with these forbidding florae, drawing a knife and attempting to saw through some of the stems. He couldn't be sure from where he was standing, but he thought he saw that she cut herself once on the thorns, or perhaps with her knife. She cursed a bit. Finishing up, she wrapped the blooms in a scrap of cloth and took them with her, departing by way of the hedge. He knew she was off to sell them during the coming day. He knew because it was Ginny.

So that is where she gets her flowers, thought Henry, who had been able to watch this happening unnoticed. Unnoticed by the young Miss Flowers, anyhow. As he'd lingered to take in this scene (and, afterward, to ponder the dire immediacy and depth of the troubles facing Madge and Ginny that it signified), someone had spotted him. Stealing up stealthily from behind was a man whose thick neck and massive jaw served to make his narrow squint and upcurled lip all the more menacing. He was rapidly closing the distance between himself and the upper-class gentleman. To this sneaking ne'er-do-well, the latter likely appeared well-off, a few decades older than himself, and, most importantly, oblivious to his presence, if not outright lost.

In other words...*easy prey.*

Suddenly, Henry found himself immobilised. He was caught completely by surprise, his hands forced behind his back as some unseen person got him into a firm hold. He was knocked to the ground a moment later, a heavy knee pressing sharply down on him between the shoulder blades. He squirmed ineffectually, trying to get out from underneath his unknown assailant. A low voice then commanded him brusquely:

'Don't move.' It added, 'You give me the smallest lick o' trouble, and you ain't goin' to be around tomorrow to regret it.'

The doctor stilled. The brawny mugger atop him began frisking his victim's pockets. Henry's mind raced as he wondered what to do. He knew the pockets were utterly empty; Madge had used whatever their contents might have been to support Ginny and herself long ago. There was no pocket-watch, either, which was probably a prize this robber was eager for. No, Henry had nothing save the suit itself. He feared how this man who had him at his mercy would react when he eventually found out. There was a good chance it wouldn't be pretty. The doctor feared for his safety. He had to think of something, and quickly, too, for only one pocket had not yet been searched.

'I took this suit from a dead man,' Henry suddenly interjected. (In its own way, he reasoned, what he said was true.) 'You won't find anything, for I have nothing and neither did he, not even his poor life. Oh, he was most upset with me for taking his clothes, sir, but I had need of them because I was cold. He was cold, too, but then, he had already died, poor soul, and all dead men are cold—that is, if they haven't just died a few minutes before, of course. I mean to say, their bodies are cold. Their souls might be rather hot, depending upon where they go.'

'Shut up afore I pop you one,' warned his attacker, who was, in truth, a mite confused. He doubted this man was anything but rich. Judging by his little speech, he was, apparently, quite eccentric, to boot. Unless he *was* some homeless man, touched in the head, who really *had* stolen clothes from a corpse... But, no, he looked too clean for that and spoke too properly. Eccentric old bastard was probably just trying to wriggle out of giving him anything. Probably had a hidden pocket inside his suit jacket where he was hiding everything of value.

In one swift move, he flipped his happenstance prey over, immediately pinning the doctor in this new position. Reaching inside the odd fellow's jacket, the robber felt along the lining, searching for the subtle slash he knew must be there.

Henry continued talking at him. 'Oh, please, my dear chap, you must let me go; 'tis a matter of grave importance.'

'I'll bet,' the mugger muttered sarcastically, and then struck the doctor across the face.

The right side of Henry's jaw started swelling not a few seconds later. Still, he felt he had to keep trying. This gambit was, quite possibly, his only chance.

'Please, sir, I beg of you! The Queen is depending upon me, and if I cannot save her, I fear she is lost to all.'

'What the bloody 'ell are you talkin' about?' The mugger's brow furrowed in confusion, his top lip raised—half in impatience and half in disgust. His hands continued to frisk Henry's jacket.

'Her Majesty, my good man—Her Majesty is in grave danger! I have been personally selected by the House of Lords to go to Malta and save her, before Napoleon can do her any further harm! Now, I beseech you, let me go! The fate of the nation rides upon the safety of our Queen!' He let his upper teeth show ever so slightly, while giving such a keen and piercing stare that the wide whites above his irises were clearly visible even in these dimly lit surroundings.

'Mother o' God—are you off in the 'ead?' The thug relaxed his hold a little, in shock. He couldn't believe his wretched luck...

'That is exactly what those fools at the hospital kept insisting, the Devil take the lot of them! Pricking me with needles, tying me to the bloody bed... They could not see the importance of my mission! They would not let me out, even though I informed them of the graveness of the situation with regard to Her Majesty's safety! They were probably spies for Napoleon himself! And the pudding there was absolutely terrible...'

Just then, he began shaking with such sudden violence that his assailant thought himself atop a bucking stallion. The mugger drew back from him by reflex. For a second or two, he simply watched, mystified; his would-be victim writhed upon the cold, damp ground, teeth locked together and eyes staring wildly in what appeared to be a fit or seizure.

'Bloody lunatic!' the thwarted robber cursed. To vent his surprise and frustration, he gave Henry a swift kick in the side. Then he took off in the other direction, aiming to get far away from the scene of such madness and the attention it stood to attract.

As soon as Henry was sure the man was out of sight, he ceased his theatrics. Though he by no means wished to be egotistical, he was passing proud of the performance he'd just given. It had, quite possibly, saved his life. He'd managed to escape the encounter with no more than a swollen jaw and a bruised underbelly. He thanked the stars he'd been lucky enough to encounter so many people with such a range of illnesses, mental and physical, during his years of medical practice. It seemed he had particular skill at mimicking the symptoms of epilepsy, as familiar as he was with them.

After waiting a few minutes—just to be sure the mugger was gone and wouldn't notice his departure—he took his leave, walking quickly and with a much better awareness of his surroundings.

CHAPTER FOUR

Henry arrived right at dawn, the first rays of the sun slimly making their way down, filtering palely through the narrow gaps between the neighbourhood's tall, trim, tastefully spartan houses. This was Gaunt Street. John's street.

Spying his friend's home, he cautiously made his way up to the door. He wondered how he would be received. He'd composed a brace of letters before certain events had been set in motion, and had left them sitting unassumingly on a corner of his own desk. But had they come to John's attention? His friend had breached the room so rapidly, it seemed, breaking down the sturdy door with record speed, bursting into Henry's private study much more quickly than he would've thought possible. And then...well, the doctor did not know what had happened next, as he'd not been around long after John had ruined the door.

Assuming the attorney had found the letter meant for him—which was the likely thing, as it had theretofore escaped destruction and John was an observant man—what had he thought of it? Did he believe its contents? Did he think Harry mad? Did he deduce that his friend had faked death, in order to keep his good name intact? All this and more ran through the doctor's mind as he stood there, preparing to knock, at his old friend's doorstep. He almost lost his nerve. Finally, however, steeling his resolve, he raised his hand and reached out to lift the knocker. He brought it down decidedly, knocking thrice, the sounds from the ensuing collisions echoing firmly as they reverberated down the sombre street. Come what may, he would face John. He had to. He could only hope for the best...

A few moments later, someone opened the door. It was Mr Guest, the lawyer's head clerk. A look of surprise leapt across his face as he laid eyes on his employer's missing friend.

'Docto—' he tried to exclaim, but Henry cut him off abruptly. He didn't desire to be rude; he simply dared not suffer Mr Guest creating a ruckus of any kind. His future course of action depended largely on John's reaction, on whether he believed—and could forgive—Harry's story or not. Additionally, this neighbourhood was home mainly to elderly folk, most of them early risers who would be getting up just about now. For these reasons, he hurriedly shushed the well-meaning clerk and hastily made his way inside the house, too desperate to stand on ceremony.

'I must speak with John,' Henry informed him urgently. 'It is a matter of utmost importance.'

'Very well, sir,' Mr Guest returned, trying to take the doctor's unexpected appearance here in stride. 'I shall send a servant for him.' (This he did.) Guest regarded the visitor a moment. He shook his head, commenting, 'But this is wondrous strange. We all thought—well, rightly, sir, we didn't know what to think.'

I should imagine, the physician mused inwardly.

'But it is good you are alive, doctor,' John's man continued. 'My employer will be most relieved. I believe he feared the worst.'

This last statement troubled Henry. Had his friend not seen the confession after all? If such were the case... A sudden mental yelp of alarm flashed through his skull—had the police found it? That would undo everything he'd set his hopes on!

Oh, God, thought Henry, panic threatening to permeate him through. *Oh, God... What am I to do?*

Just then, John appeared near the top of the stairs. The way the staircase was constructed, there was a slight overhang to the balustrade to the right of where the steps terminated on the upper floor—a sort of miniature balcony. It was here that John stood, looking down at Mr Guest, whom he was fairly surprised to see at this hour of the morning. It also followed that, as his friend Harry chanced to be directly beneath said 'balconette', the overhang prevented John from noticing the doctor's presence. Nor was the latter aware of the attorney's timely arrival, though he did mark how Mr Guest suddenly ceased their conversation, only to look upward, somewhere over Henry's head. Guest paid him no heed at all, now that John was on the scene. Harry wondered what was up—quite literally—but said nothing, for the moment.

'Guest, what on earth are you doing here at this hour?!' John more exclaimed than enquired. 'It's barely dawn!'

The doctor only half-listened to the head clerk's reply—something about papers for a particular property transfer case, though any fool could see the man was worried about his employer after the strange events of last night and more than a little curious what had transpired. The doctor thought instead on what to do now (no clue), how he would answer John's inevitable enquiries (the truth?), whether escape were a viable option (too late), and most frighteningly, that the police might've got their mitts on his personal confession (good God).

His time for further reflection on these vital questions was cruelly cut short. The clerk, in an attempt to divert John's hard probing from himself, suddenly changed the subject with the unexpected news: John's dear, good friend was here, and wasn't that just grand?

Oh, bloody Hell, thought Henry. His time had come. He steeled himself as best he could. Then, putting on a smile, he emerged into John's range of vision. Standing at the end of the stairs, he prepared to ask the lawyer how he'd been, or perhaps remark that his appearing here must surely come as a great surpri—

'Harry!' John half-yelped, catching him completely unprepared. 'God's blood! I don't believe it!' He hurried stiffly down the stairs.

Henry, who was rather in shock at his friend's uncharacteristic display, could not so much as move. John was an outwardly pious man, and the doctor hadn't heard him curse like this since their school days. He was also normally reserved—laconic, even—unless picking an argument apart. It took Harry by surprise when his old friend, upon reaching the bottom of the staircase, clapped him warmly on the shoulder. The lawyer beamed with happiness, excitement, relief, and not a little perplexity.

'I thought you lost,' he declared, 'especially after reading your case statement.'

So he has *read it, then*, Henry noted to himself.

'I did not see how anything but ill must have become of you,' continued John, 'one way or the other.' He noticed Guest and turned toward him. 'Mr Guest, I ask you again, what on earth are you doing here at this hour? And I would appreciate a real answer this time,' he said bluntly enough, all but impaling the chief clerk with his formidable gaze.

'I...I had wanted to get a head start on the Islington case, sir, and had need of the papers,' Guest explained. 'I believe they are still in your desk and, as I did not wish to disturb you, I awaited your awakening—thus.' He gestured at the seating area just right of the bottom of the stairs.

In fact, Hubert Guest had been concerned over the state of his longtime employer. The latter had left the previous evening in a restive frame of mind, after a butler had come to the door and entreated John to investigate the wellbeing of one of the lawyer's closest friends. John still had not returned by the time Guest, who was in the habit of working late, had gathered up his effects and left for home. The look on the butler's face had worried Hubert, and he thought he'd overheard the phrase 'foul play' mentioned at least once. But apparently, everything was alright now... Guest was glad. John was a decent enough sort—a bit brusque around the edges, but that was hardly unexpected in an employer. And he paid well. Good to know he hadn't become involved in a murder or anything, trying to help his friend.

'Well, I'm certainly awake now,' John asserted, glancing at the miraculously-not-dead Henry. He then resumed to Guest, 'The office door is unlocked. You'll find the key to my desk in its usual place.'

'Very good,' Guest mumbled as he set off.

John turned back to Harry. He honestly was not sure what to think, a rare occurrence for the lawyer. His friend obviously had not been murdered, but what, then, *had* transpired? If Henry hadn't been forced to write that letter by his would-be murderer... well, it could mean one of two things. The most logical explanation was that poor old Harry had gone mad, or at least been in a fit of some sort or else under the influence of drugs while writing the damned thing. The second possibility, far less rational, was that Henry had written the truth, and that truth was far stranger than he or anyone might ever have imagined...

He decided to proceed carefully, lest the first model prove true and his friend turn out to be 'not all there', mentally speaking. Yet John did not wish to let on that this was what he was doing.

'So then, Henry,' he began, aiming to act as naturally as possible, given the circumstances, 'no doubt you realise I have many questions. And you, I hope, can provide me at least some of their answers.' He paused, then remarked wryly, 'You look rather well, for a dead man.'

'Well, I should imagine,' responded the doctor with a mildly amused look. He then asserted humbly, 'I count myself very lucky indeed. I have had a lesson—O God, John, what a lesson I have had!—but I digress.' He looked affirmingly at the attorney. 'Yes, I am sure you doubtless have a great many questions. And I intend to answer them fully.'

More to himself, 'I should have done so from the outset,' he uttered, then spoke once more to his friend, 'but I thought...I felt it was a secret—a burden—I could not share with anyone, not even my closest of friends. You have read the confession, John. I knew it was too fantastic for belief,' he continued, 'and, what is more, I did not wish to trouble you. It was a situation of my own making; I found it shameful, and yet...' Here Henry broke off, concluding only in his mind, *and yet a willing slave to it.*

John could tell his friend was frankly overcome, seeing as Harry couldn't even find strength to finish his sentence. Additionally, John was now more secure in the opinion that poor Henry might indeed have gone mad, or at least have trouble with occasional fits of madness, judging by how flustered he appeared. What was more, it seemed the chap actually believed that foolish 'confession' (or, to the lawyer's mind, 'case statement') of his. He had written it of his own accord, the heartfelt, pitiable ramblings of a madman, apologies and explanations from a mind tormented by its own imagined guilt and the nonsensical ramifications thereof.

Poor Harry, thought John. Well, he had best look after his old friend, he supposed. Perhaps try to get him to come round. Maybe he simply needed someone to talk to. John had had a number of friends and acquaintances over the years, many of whom had been caught in their own downward spirals, and most had confided in him to some degree or other. He was, after all, a rather good listener. His rational perspective, beneficially distanced from their particular and sundry situations, had often provided if not solutions, then at least some insights that usually proved helpful. And, if not, these people still profited from taking a load off their souls. Truth be told, John found them rather amusing. Not that he didn't care about them—merely that their thoughts and responses to their own (often self-created) circumstances intrigued him. Had he not been a lawyer, he might've explored this almost scientific bent, perhaps becoming an alienist. His mind was always working.

Right now, it was working on how best to proceed. He settled on taking Henry to the withdrawing room, out of earshot of any servants or clerks, there to hear the good doctor lay bare his heart and see if any remedy mightn't be found. He hoped so, in his own detachedly determined way. John had already lost one dear friend this year, seen death and despair eat him through, only to eventually help the other pallbearers lower him into the ground. He did not wish to bear witness as madness laid claim his other. If anything could be done, he would do it.

To the drawing room, then, he resolved.

***

John bade Henry go in first. Entering the room, the doctor took a seat on a fine leather sofa that ran parallel to the left-hand wall. John followed, settling into a large chair opposite. The furniture was of simple design but very good quality, rich brown-red leather softening a frame of stark, polished mahogany. Straight ahead, to Henry's left and the right of John, brilliant sunshine made its way through wood-rimmed windowpanes, the low angle of its trajectory rendering the two men silhouettes to anyone standing in the doorway.

A servant brought them tea, which Henry gratefully accepted. After she had left, John locked the door, making it clear that this was a private conversation and they were not to be disturbed unless it was sorely urgent.

There was a brief silence, then:

'Interesting suit you have on, Harry,' remarked the lawyer, marking his friend's comically nostalgic clothes. 'I've not seen one that style for years.'

'Ah, this,' said Henry, looking down as if just noticing his odd apparel again. 'I admit these raiments are a touch strange. But then, my entire experience recently has been thus, last night proving no exception whatsoever. Such an odd array of circumstances, John! The likelihood of what has transpired—any of it—ever actually occurring, especially in conjunction...' He trailed off, the sheer improbability of it all beginning to sink in, becoming slowly, truly real to him.

John let him stay off inside himself for a small while, but shortly broke in, trying ever so subtly to manoeuvre his friend back on track. (And, though patient, he was also highly curious.)

'And what might those circumstances be?' he cut in, Harry's previous thoughts evaporating as the lawyer commanded his attention. 'You haven't yet told me how it is you came to be here. I was at a loss, you know. What was I to make of it? After we broke down the door—'

'We?' interrupted a confused Henry.

'Your butler and I,' answered John.

'Ah.'

'Speaking of which, do your staff know of your fate?'

'No, I—I came directly here. You are my closest friend, John, as well as my attorney, and I was wondering...well, naturally I wanted to tell you what transpired; that, any friend would do. However, I had hoped that you might perhaps counsel me on how best to proceed, once I explain everything.'

John was immensely relieved. Harry was showing quite a bit of sense. Perhaps he wasn't mad after all—at least, not all the time—and a reasonable explanation would be forthcoming.

He was right on the first account, yet sorely, sorely wrong about the latter.

***

Even after Henry'd told John everything, his old friend still did not believe his account. Of course, the lawyer never intentionally let on that this was the case, but Henry could tell. Harry didn't know exactly how he knew but, somehow, know it he did, as surely as he knew his own name. Perhaps it came from being friends for so long, or maybe he was just good at reading people (a useful skill for a doctor). In any case, Henry could see he was getting nowhere in his efforts to convince the attorney, even though he'd answered all John's questions with the absolute, none-too-pretty, honest-to-goodness truth. Even when he pointed out the letter, which John surely must have perused, written by their mutual friend Hastie (so recently deceased), an account which corroborated Harry's story in every aspect—even then, John remained immutably unswayed. Not that the attorney said anything to such effect, of course.

For his own part, John had formulated a theory—more of a working model, really—that took all the known facts into account and integrated them into one sane, highly sensible, overarching framework. With this larger picture laid out, yet more pieces suddenly fell into place and, in a flash, John understood all that had transpired: It was obvious to him that Henry, in his scientific studies, had taken to experimenting with chemicals which caused delusion, and had inadvertently exposed himself to massive quantities thereof. This was no doubt the reason for his sporadic but recurring reclusiveness this past year; even when hallucinating, it seemed Harry still had the good sense to keep himself away from the eyes of others...most of the time. On one occasion, however, it seemed his drug-induced insanity had got the better of him. In a fit of madness wherein he still retained the majority of his mental functions, he had written a letter to their mutual friend, Hastie, asking him with dire urgency to go and fetch a drawer of his chemicals. The contents therein surely induced madness in whomever they came in contact with, as had evidently happened to Hastie, judging from his now-departed friend's impossible letter and unexpected death shortly thereafter. The man had fallen prey to a hallucination, no doubt, and a gruesome one at that—one that took all the right and natural laws of science, God, and medicine, and cruelly, smugly twisted them beyond all recognition. John wagered these phantasms had driven Hastie to an early grave. Small wonder, then, that Henry had been so altered—on and off—this past year or two. It was only by pure providence the doctor hadn't committed suicide! And here was John, Henry's so-called friend, unable to see the situation for what it was this entire time!

Well, Harry had asked for his advice and his aid, and for the lawyer to do anything but offer these at this point was patently unthinkable. For starters:

'Henry, I realise that, as a physician and a chemist, your experiments took on special importance to you. Yet I conclude they have proved most unhealthful, and would suggest you give them up entirely. The bad far outweighs the good.'

Harry was shocked and relieved at the same time, to hear John say these things. It seemed his friend believed him after all! He could not understand how he had misread the man so completely, and after knowing him all these years, too...

'I concur,' Henry agreed with him. 'I concur with much conviction; I desire never again to lay eyes upon those horrid phials, powders, and concoctions. As you say, the bad does far outweigh the good. I shall close up my laboratory and never touch the stuff again, I swear to God.' He was surprised at his own adamance but glad of it all the same. This was good. This was very good.

For John's part, he found much satisfaction in his friend's reply. Time away from those strange tinctures of his was apparently already doing the doctor some good. Grand.

***

'Here is what we shall tell the papers, Harry,' began the lawyer (for he was sure the London media would be all over his friend's ordeal). 'Your butler approached me last night, fearing something was amiss and that there might even have been foul play against you. Concerned for your welfare, I accompanied him back to your home, where we found the blackguard holed up in your laboratory. As he had barricaded the door against us and we feared for your safety, we had no choice but to break down said door. The madman had obviously lost all reason due to exposure to those harmful chemicals of yours. He took to suicide, and lay dead on the floor when we came in. We found you locked within the cellar of the operating theatre, where your adversary had kept you for several days while trying to get you to sign over all of your fortune to him. As he slipped ever further into delusion, he slowly forgot his original purpose in imprisoning you; he even began to think he *was* you, poorly impersonating your voice from behind the laboratory door—that's what tipped off the butler. Meanwhile, you were left to rot in the cellar.'

Henry nodded. Everything made sense so far.

'When they ask you, as they inevitably will, why you let such a villain into your home in the first place,' John continued, 'you will explain that he threatened to harm the widow Denman and her young granddaughter'—for Harry had told the attorney about his chance meeting with these two—'about whom you cared deeply out of respect for your old mentor. Attempting to buy time in your search for a way to restore the original Denman fortune to them and thereby take them out of harm's way without hurting Mrs Denman's pride, you placated this man, opening your home to him, even writing him cheques on occasion—effectively saying, "Nice doggie," all the while trying to find a rock with which to fend him off. Unfortunately, the man became impatient and took to drastic action which you did not foresee.'

'That's good,' said Henry, in awe of his friend's wily reweaving of the facts. 'That's very good.'

'Of course,' remarked John matter-of-factly. 'Thank you.'

'No trouble at all,' replied the lawyer with a small shrug and the barest hint of a smile.

***

And so things fell out fairly much the way John had anticipated. The papers had a field day covering the doctor's miraculous return; Londoners were shocked to learn how easily and thoroughly the suicidal madman had insinuated himself into the life of the upstanding physician. No doubt many privately wondered what they would do if they found themselves in a similar situation. Of course, unlike Henry's apparent case, most of these feared blackmail arising from their own unwholesome deeds, not out of concern for the relatives of a late, discredited mentor. Though the populace did nothing to improve the lot of Ginny and her grandmother, afraid that to do so might implicate them somehow with the late Dr Denman, a significant portion of the townsfolk admired Henry's bravery in doing so. Some few did question his sincerity in the matter, thinking that he, like themselves, must've had dubious motives for any such seemingly unselfish actions. But the rest took his statement at face value. After all, he had long been a philanthropist, often providing medical care to the sick and needy who could not otherwise afford it. In this respect, he genuinely followed Denman's praiseworthy example.

Much ado was made about the crazed, deceased, would-be murderer, and how close Henry had come to an early grave. Several newsmen pressed the police to let them see the body of this madman, but it was nowhere to be found. One reporter asked the doctor if he was sure the scoundrel was really dead, to which Henry replied, 'Oh, yes, I am quite certain. He shall never trouble anyone again, that I promise you.'

John took this moment to change the subject and direct the journalist's attention to other matters. The lawyer had suspected his friend might've killed his captor—in self-defence, no doubt, but killed him all the same—and this latest show of adamance on Harry's part now verified the attorney's suspicions. Not that John thought less of him for it—after all, in Henry's shoes, he likely would've done the same—but the lawyer did not wish to give the media men any more opportunity to figure out the secret than was absolutely necessary.

The police, to cover up their own ineptitude, eventually told the press that the mad criminal's body had been passed on to some unknown group of medical students or other, there to benefit the young minds of science, before anyone had realised whose body it was or how sensational a story it would turn out to be involved with.

A few childish London anatomy students had a heyday with this information—at least, when their instructors were not in the room. Across the city, exchanges not unlike the following took place:

'Haha! Look at this! It's the eye of a madman!' sneered one young man, poking at the cornea of some anonymous cadaver.

'That's nothing,' declared another youth. '*I'll* dissect his *brain*,' he asserted in his best rendition of a creepy, demented-sounding voice.

'I have you all beat,' trumpeted a third lad, trying not to grin. The others stopped and looked at him.

'What are you on about?' one asked.

With a triumphant flourish, the smaller fellow gestured to an organ that put all the other students' claims to shame. Beaming, he pointed out:

'Look at his *unmentionable*! Imagine the places *this* has been!'

Gasps and laughter ensued, erupting suddenly from all assembled. Yet these were quickly, inexplicably cut short. His classmates appeared to look at the apparent 'winner' of the impromptu contest with a mixture of shock and trepidation. He had no idea why…that is, until he heard a stern voice from behind him.

'*Mister Butterstotch*,' boomed the instructor with such intensity that it nearly knocked him down, 'Cease your foolishness this instant!'

The chap blanched. He knew his parents were going to be really steamed when they heard about this…

CHAPTER FIVE

After the media hubbub died down a bit, life gradually began to return to normal for Henry. The gauntness vanished from his frame, leaving no trace of its passage; he became hale and hearty once more. In contrast to his former reclusiveness, he was once again seen out and about, helping his patients, giving lectures, volunteering his time, going on strolls through Regent's Park, attending—and hosting—a great many parties, and generally enjoying the pleasures of a regular, upstanding life, with many a good time spent in the company of his friends and acquaintances. He shut down his lab, just as he had promised John. Aside from this, his activities fell back to fairly much the way they had been before his ordeal...with one exception: He was abstinent in every way possible, eschewing relations even with himself. For, although he did not really believe he would once more fall prey to his previous, strange malady (seeing as the chances of contracting it again were practically non-existent), he thought it prudent to take the high road and avoid tempting fate altogether.

Yet, as time wore on, he began to feel the urgings of this most natural, human need nagging at him more and more frequently, with ever-increasing intensity. He struggled internally to leave this unwholesome part of himself behind for good, attempting, by his impeccable behaviour, to rid himself of these unwelcome longings. But such was a fool's charade. He felt as he felt, knew what he craved, and could no more change his state than a grieving widow could render herself euphoric simply by willing it so.

Thus it was that, some months after his initial reintroduction to society, Harry found himself wandering a lonely little bystreet in one of London's seedier quarters. It was very late in the evening—or early in the morning, depending upon how one chose to look at it—and the good doctor had just come from a rather dull party, a soiree thrown to celebrate the umpteenth wedding anniversary of some high-society couple who didn't really love each other anyway. With all the marriages of convenience that took place, and with so many women (or, more accurately, so many women's parents) who would have sought him out just for his fortune, was it any wonder he'd never taken a wife?

And yet he could not get rid of these blasted desires of his! It was unbecoming for a man of his age. After all, it was already mid-August; come the thirteenth of November, he would find himself a ripe old fifty-two. (Never mind that he looked as if he were still in his forties...) Much too old for such...*undignified* pleasures.

Yet here he was. He stopped across the street from a brothel, trying to blend into the stonework of the alleyway behind him as he wrestled with himself over what or what not to do.

Damn it all! he thought. *Am I never to change?* The whole dilemma seemed ludicrous. He knew what was right, knew what he had to—*should*—do. And still, even as the thought crossed his mind, his gaze wandered over the women in the window across the street, the yellow, warm lighting of the dingy little establishment illuminating them, drawing his attention to all their most...*appealing* features.

Something else caught his eye. At first, he wasn't sure why—he'd come here tonight seeking women, not anything worse—but he found himself unable to take his eyes off a particular fellow who had just ducked into the bordello. The man moved from one window to another, apparently taking stock of his options before finally heading over and talking figures with the madam. The gent appeared to be in his early forties—a full decade Henry's junior—and wore a cape, a fine hat, and a peculiar, self-satisfied smirk the doctor had seen on only one particular person in his over-a-half-century of life: Richard Falstaff.

Huh, thought Harry, the surprise of it hitting him as soon as he realised who it was. *I search for the man the entire summer, never once able to get ahold of him, and then here—*

and now—I simply chance to run into him? One part of him felt like shaking his head in disgust at the irony. Another coolly reflected that finding Dick in a place like this was not all that surprising. Still another threatened to snicker at the perhaps unintended pun (a bit of impatient gaiety that the doctor found unseemly). Finally, Henry was mostly just grateful to have caught the chap at all. He had wanted to talk to him about Madge and Ginny's misfortunes, to see if he might unharden, even slightly, a heart so full of envy it had condoned the downfall of a well-respected doctor and the misery this caused his widow and grandchild. And if Harry could not persuade him, then he might at least fish for information. Madge, when he had talked with her, had expressed confusion over Dr Denman's not having written a new will, one which would've allowed the woman he cared most about to receive her fair due, rather than leaving such things to the law's nearest-male-relative default (by which Dick inherited nearly everything).

Well, decision made, then. Henry crossed the street and entered in the house of ill repute.

***

'Well, if it ain't the doctor!' exclaimed the madam when Henry made his way in. 'What a pleasant surprise.'

He smiled. Damned if it wasn't good to be back.

"'S been a long time, 'enry,' she continued. 'We was beginnin' to think you'd forgotten about us.'

'Not in the least, my dear madam,' he pronounced, adding, 'Though I have been rather busy as of late, as I'm sure the papers have made everyone all too well aware.'

'Get tired of those stuffy ol' excuses for parties, didja?'

'Quite,' he affirmed with a nod, raising his eyebrows as he did so in a gesture of utter agreement coupled with an unspoken, *You have no idea...*

'Well, you've come to the right place, doc,' the elder woman asserted. 'Gents like you's always welcome 'ere. Ain't that right, girls?' she asked, turning to a bevy of beauties (or near approximations thereof), some buxom, some not so, who all nodded or spoke in the affirmative in answer to the madam's rhetorical query.

'So, 'oo'll it be tonight?' she enquired, turning her attention back to the client. 'If you want to start off slow—you know, ease yourself back into things, as it were—'eather there's a decent pick.' She pointed to a girl of about fourteen that Harry had never seen before. 'Joined us a week ago, she did, and she's learnin' fairly quick.'

'No, thank you, madam,' he replied politely, looking at the young lady, 'though I'm sure she is quite lovely.'

He was about to continue, but the madam, who thought he had finished, cut in. 'Right, then, of course, doc. 'Ow stupid of me. 'S been over 'alf a year since you come 'ere last; you must be just rarin' to go. If I might, sir, I'd recommend the twins—Lauren and Laura's their names. They're awful good, if I do say so meself, and,' she added as she gave him a knowing wink, 'there's two of 'em, if you catch me drift.'

'Thank you, madam,' he said to her, 'but, again, I must decline. I was actually wondering—' he began, taking a glance around the place.

'Ah, you're lookin' for Jeanine; that's it, isn't it?' the madam surmised, regarding the doctor with a look of realisation.

'Well, I had wondered where she was,' Henry put in (for he had been this beauty's quasi-regular, in the past), intending to continue with a query as to the whereabouts of Dr Richard Falstaff.

The madam beat him to the punch. 'Oh, she's busy with Doc Dick just now, but I'm sure she'll 'ave plenty left for you. Girl's got stamina,' she asserted, giving the doctor a mischievous look, 'as I'm sure you know.' Harry smiled despite himself. His grin broadened when the madam whispered conspiratorially, 'An' Dick don't, so they oughta be out shortly.'

He informed the elder woman that he would wait, and ordered a drink to pass the time. It was port, not brandy—he wanted to take the edge off, yet still have his wits about him when he conversed with Falstaff. He looked forward to a fling with Jeanine afterward. Her soft, supple curves, her melodious voice saying wonderfully indecent things to him in French as he melted pleasurably into her... Yes, it had been a while. He was going to enjoy this very much.

First things first, though. Work before pleasure. (Wasn't that always the way...?) He couldn't be sure he'd be able to get ahold of Dr Falstaff at any other time, so he waited patiently in the hall by the door to the bedroom wherein the pair had vanished, intending to speak with Dick as soon as they finished, while the oh-so-fortuitous chance still presented itself.

Henry had only half-finished his port when the door cracked open. He quickly downed the rest, setting his empty glass on a nearby stand. The door then opened further, revealing a rather self-satisfied Falstaff. His expression changed to surprise and a pinch of confusion as he noticed Harry, then morphed into smugness as he realised he might later use this chance encounter to his advantage: one of the finest, most upstanding physicians in London (not unlike Harold Denman had once been), caught at a common whorehouse! Of course, Henry had seen him here, too, but Falstaff wagered the elder man had more to lose.

'Dr Falstaff, I presume,' Henry began.

'Shhh!' the other man shushed him, a scowl of impertinence creasing his features. 'They don't know my surname here.'

They did now, judging by the way the madam, who was at present behind the counter and just out of Dick's line of vision, looked up and away, as if to pointedly demonstrate that she had heard nothing.

'Terribly sorry,' the good doctor apologised in a lowered tone. 'I wasn't aware.'

'Apparently,' Falstaff retorted with a look of annoyance.

Oh dear, thought Harry. Things were not getting off to a good start, not in the least...

'Now, if you don't mind,' the younger man continued, 'I'm going to have a glass of brandy.' He made as if to move past Henry.

'I hope you'll forgive my forwardness,' the other put in, cutting Dick off from leaving as he did so, 'but I was rather hoping I might speak to you in private. It is a matter of some—no, I would even say, of *great*—import, and not a little urgency.' For Harry knew the widow Denman and her granddaughter might, any day, run out of funds completely. And Madge was still too damnably proud and stubborn to accept even his help—he, who owed them so much!

'Might we discuss this at some other time?' Falstaff nasalised in vexation. Why the bloody hell was this chap so intent on bothering him? He hoped he wasn't being propositioned—not by a man his own age or more, anyway...

'I am at a loss for what other time might suffice,' replied Henry. 'The matter I have to discuss with you is, as I have said, quite private, and to arrange to meet later would make a separate occasion of it. Such would draw suspicion.' The philanthropic doctor was willing to let Falstaff's reputation remain intact, even better it, and to support the widow and Ginny himself, so long as Dick made a show of generosity (whether he was sincere or not) and was the one who physically gave the money to Madge. Yes, he was even willing to go so far as to pay the man—generously—for his part in this little charade. Madge, Henry knew, simply would not accept assistance from anyone under any other terms.

To Falstaff's ears, however, it sounded as if the elder physician were intimating something of an entirely different (and questionable) nature—especially given the fellow's insistence on holding their conversation now and in private, lest it 'draw suspicion'.

Noticing the other's hesitation, Harry added, 'I assure you, I shall make it worth your while.'

This did not help matters any. (Dick did, however, take note of the fact that Henry was apparently a homosexual, keeping the information mentally 'on file' should he ever have need of it to manipulate or blackmail the elder, wealthier, more respected medical practitioner.)

Falstaff decided to indulge him, if only to let Henry hang himself by his own words. Dick could then coerce him at his leisure and threaten to tell the authorities he'd been propositioned if the elder gent didn't do as he demanded.

'Very well,' the plotter seemingly relented. 'We will speak. Only, let me finish my business for the night here first.'

'Yes, of course,' Harry readily complied. What luck! He'd been afraid the younger doctor would dismiss him entirely, but it appeared things were shaping up after all. Splendid.

And so, Dick set about concluding his affairs at the dubious establishment. He ordered a glass of brandy, then set off to some anonymous room with Heather, aiming to give the new girl a try. Meanwhile, Henry bought two glasses of cognac, one for himself and one for Jeanine (it was her favourite drink). He finished his rather quickly, welcoming the dampening of self-awareness that ensued, and retreated to a quiet, private room with the French beauty. It *had* been a while...

***

Afterward, as he lay there sleepily against her body, soft and warm, it occurred to him how very lucky he was. He had almost lost everything, including (not least) his life and himself, had come back from the brink of self-destruction, had regained his name, his friends, his fortune—*everything*—and now lay here beside a gorgeous, supple, auburn-haired woman he enjoyed spending nights with. Yes, life was good—*very* good—and he was utterly content...except for one small, niggling thing: his conscience, which had only just now begun to resurface as the alcohol and event wore gradually off. It chattered annoyingly in the back of his head, its yammering thankfully vague and muted as of yet.

He knew it would grow louder, though. It always did. Things always happened this way.

For the moment, he lay there in a particular point on this cycle—the all-too-familiar feeling of the animal within him licking the chops of memory, his moralistic side a little drowsy, promising subsequent repentance but not moved to begin quite yet.

His dreamy reverie was cut short by the sound of a sudden crash, as of glass just... *sleeting* down, from the other end of the hall.

He sat up suddenly, ears pricked, as did Jeanine, her sea-green eyes darting about in mild alarm, as if searching for the source of the sound. Harry could tell by her reaction that this was a different class of crash than the kind caused by overenthusiastic drunkards who unintentionally handled their drinking glasses a touch too roughly.

A second smash ensued, followed sharply by a scream.

Fearing someone might be hurt, Henry hurriedly threw on his clothes and dashed out into the hall. Jeanine began to re-dress as well, but she had significantly more to put on—not the least of which was her corset—and in truth, didn't want to be involved in whatever the trouble was.

From the other end of the hall, Harry saw Dick and Heather emerge, the former attempting to yank the latter back into their room. The girl was putting up quite a fight, and Falstaff was a smaller-than-average man, but she was still just fourteen and could not hold out forever.

The madam arrived at the scene the same time Henry did.

''Ere then, what's this about?' she demanded, looking sternly at the two involved.

''E's tryin' to do unnatural things to me!' Heather cried. 'Un-Christian things, mum, things what just ain't right to do to anyone!' She seemed shaken, fear and shame unmistakable as she looked about with haunted eyes.

'What's this, then?' the madam asked Falstaff. 'You ain't gone and 'urt 'er, 'ave you?'

'Madam, I am insulted! I am certainly not that sort of fellow!' Dick returned with an acrimonious expression.

'You'd best 'ope not,' the proprietress shot back. Then, on a calmer note, she explained, 'No 'arm meant to you, Doc Dick, but you got to understand, we 'ad a man in 'ere not too long ago—'bout a year afore you started frequentin' the place—and 'e 'urt Charlotte—she was our other Frenchie, you see—'e bruised 'er up real bad, 'e did. I banned 'im from comin' 'ere after that, but it didn't make no difference to Charlotte. Poor girl stowed away back to France not long after.'

'An amusing tale, I'm sure,' Falstaff said, rolling his eyes. 'One that has *absolutely nothing* to do with *me*, woman.'

'Look, I'm sorry if I gave you offence, Doc,' the madam put in. 'You're a payin' client, just like anyone else, and Lord knows I ain't 'ere to run off business. But I can't afford to lose me girls, neither. So, all's I'm sayin' is, round 'ere, it just pays to be real careful, 'specially what with what's 'appened in the past.' She turned to Harry, knowing he would likely back her up. 'Ain't that right, doc?'

'Y...yes, I should say so,' he agreed, then swallowed hard. 'Particularly given such... such a precedent as the one you mentioned.' He'd had no idea Charlotte had left for good. No wonder she was absent tonight! *God*, he thought, feeling the bottom drop out of his stomach, *it truly has been a long while since I've been here.*

The madam and Dick resumed their discussion, Henry paying them only vague attention as he pondered how very final repercussions could be. Charlotte was gone. He knew the cad who had hit her, knew how unforgiving he could be, how quick to anger—

''E came at me from behind!'

What? thought Harry, suddenly snapping back to the real world as the girl's exclamation broke abruptly into his ruminations. Not able to help himself, he turned his attention back to the conversation—or, more accurately, argument—going on among Heather, Dick, and the madam (all of whom seemed to have forgotten Henry's presence).

'But it's just un-Christian, mum! I ain't no barnyard beast!' Heather protested.

The madam, relieved to find out that was all this was about, gave a short, breathy laugh.

'Oh, 'eather, dear, that's nothin' to worry about at all! You'll get used to it in no time. 'S perfectly simple.'

'And what does a whore have to worry about being un-Christian anyway?' Dick said with an impatient sneer.

'Well, she's still a bit of a child now, Doc Dick. She ain't used to quite all of our worldly ways just yet. Give 'er some time, is all. She does aim to please, even if she is a bit new at it.'

'You were wise not to charge full price for her,' Falstaff observed sourly. 'Only a fool would pay it.' As it was, he wondered if he oughtn't ask for a refund. But then he took a second look at Heather, at her comely frame, sky-blue eyes, and flower-pink dress with all its ruffles. 'Though I am willing to give her another go,' he added.

'Well, that's settled, then,' declared the madam.

Heather was clearly dejected, but tried to put on a good face.

'Might we get someone to clean this up?' Falstaff enquired, indicating his empty glass of brandy and a small, blue-and-white porcelain box, both of which lay broken on the floorboards of the frilly little bedroom.

'So that was what I heard,' said Henry softly.

'Your clumsy girl knocked them down when she jumped away from me,' Dick asserted. He wanted to make sure he wasn't liable for any expenses.

Hum, thought Harry. The whole scene seemed a bit fishy to him. He had worked with mentally disordered patients before, not a few of whom had been known to throw things about in the midst of their mad fits. The breakables presently lying on the floor looked to have undergone a similar process, judging by how many pieces there were and the angles at which the two items had shattered. Dick had thrown them at Heather, of that Henry was sure—maybe not with the intent to hit the poor girl, but definitely in her general direction, possibly at her feet. Perhaps to scare her, make her comply...

It frightened him, sometimes, that he knew so well how these men thought. Think what that said about him, after all. He shuddered to contemplate the answer.

'You alright, 'enry?' the madam broke in. 'You look a little green. Too much cognac?'

'Perhaps,' he replied, his social persona belatedly kicking back in again. He was too inwardly distractible, too reflective, that was his problem. That was the source of all his troubles. He cared too much. Take right now, for instance. He cared about this Heather girl, even though he hardly knew her. He cared enough to want to spare the young woman from any more of Dick's abominable advances, even though—and here was the ludicrous thing—he knew the lass was a whore, knew this was all just part and parcel of her profession, and that, for her own sake, the sooner she learned it, the better off she'd be.

So why, then, did he feel such relief when Falstaff said he wanted to wait to have his way with her until that particular bedroom was cleaned up (rather than occupying another one)? And how did Henry suddenly find himself intervening on the girl's behalf in case Dick changed his mind, asking Falstaff if he wouldn't mind having their discussion now, seeing as Dick had to wait anyway? What did he think he was doing? He was only delaying the inevitable, at best; at worst, he was causing the poor girl more consternation as she was forced to wait even longer for her fate, giving her all the more time to dread it.

But it was perhaps on the off-chance that he was actually giving young Heather some much-needed minutes to recover, mentally speaking, that Henry now accompanied Dick Falstaff to a vacant room, there to go over his proposition with this most disagreeable man. And, of course, Harry knew Madge and Ginny were counting on him, even if they were unaware of it.

CHAPTER SIX

'You must be daft,' Falstaff upbraided Henry, upon hearing the physician's proposal. 'What, do you think me a fool? I've no reason to get involved, no reason whatsoever.' Dick was amazed anyone would be so naïve as to ask this of him and expect anything but a negative answer, coupled with a heaping dose of sarcasm. Did the fellow honestly think he would grovel before that old bat of Denman's and her snot-nosed little guttersnipe, just for a tidy sum of cash? He had more pride than that! What was more, he already had all the money he needed—Doctor Denman's tragic demise and purloined will had seen to that—and he wasn't about to kowtow to anyone.

Of course, Dick didn't tell Henry his (incriminating) reasons. He was also a bit ticked off that the doctor had not turned out to be a homosexual. Having nothing save the fact that he had seen him at a bordello with which to blackmail the man, Falstaff counted their entire conversation as a loss, a monumental and intelligence-insulting waste of his time.

'It isn't all that ludicrous,' Henry protested, incensed at the unexpected harshness of the other's reaction. He'd known the man likely wouldn't be overly enthusiastic about the idea, but, still... Such out-and-out rejection, not to mention insults to his very intelligence...

Perhaps another strategy was in order. Trying a different tack, Henry opted for the ploy of playing on Dick's emotions and overabundant sense of pride, as appealing to his charity and then his greed had obviously failed to do the trick.

'Think of the recognition you will receive from society—particularly high society—for doing this. Why, you shall appear a bona fide hero—magnanimous, enviable, and admired by all who hear of your great deed of generosity. And all without your losing face in public whatsoever or having to spend a penny.'

'I will *never* bow down to that *bitch*,' Falstaff rebuffed, his voice dripping pure venom. 'And as for your supposed "admiration" and "envy", I'll tell you what people will say: They will think me a fool, a sentimental fool who associates himself with the lower classes.' He paused to stare directly into the doctor's emerald-green eyes, his own hazel ones glaring in challenge, then dropped the following words on Henry like so many sticks of dynamite: 'Just. Like. You.' He sneered, adding spitefully, 'And let the two of them starve. What do I care?' For the *pièce de résistance*, he finished with a smirk, 'Who knows? If that happens, I may chance to meet little "Ginny" in this very place someday. She could hardly be any worse than that Heather girl...'

Henry stood bolt upright, fuming. (This was most uncharacteristic of him.) But the impertinence! The damnable, evil arrogance! The utter lack of pity! Who did the brat think he was?

Bloody blighter! the doctor thought. *Bloody, callous, hateful little bugger! Even on my worst of days, I never—*

He suddenly felt faint, dizzy, a wave of nausea rising up from his innards and threatening to bowl him over. His palms grew sweaty, his breathing laboured.

Oh, God, was all he could manage to think. *Oh, God, no! Please, no!* He leaned on his chair for support.

He could feel it coming. One of his fits. He'd thought he had escaped this, but—

He had to get out of here—*now*. He couldn't let anyone see him like this—not like *this*. He knew what would follow.

The doctor lurched past Dick and into the door, turning the knob with an unsteady hand. He leaned against the wood, pushing out into the hall, then wobbled down the corridor as fast as he was able. His eyes began to dilate. Turning a corner, he found an empty room in the other hall, second door from the left, and stumbled in, slamming the door closed. His knees gave out from under him. As they buckled, he fell to the ground, but somehow caught the door key on his way down, the half-turn just enough to bolt it shut. He heard the satisfying 'click.' Then, knowing he was (in a manner of speaking) safe, his will finally gave out, and he let himself be overcome completely. He thrashed about on the floor, gritting his teeth, moaning in pain, his madness rising further and further to the surface till, at last, it worked its way out of him and he lay gasping on the floor, his hands taut, his brain on fire.

***

No one noticed Henry's spasms or cries. A pair in the next room was cooking up quite a storm, and the sounds of their passion drowned out every noise nearby. Dick had seen the doctor turn the corner but hadn't followed, being rather unsure what it all meant. Had he really got under the chap's skin so badly that he'd run from the room? Or had the younger physician instead witnessed the unseemly start of an epileptic seizure? He hadn't known the elder man to have this problem but, then again, one never endeavoured to make public such potentially embarrassing ailments. Society simply would not tolerate any personal weakness of that magnitude, particularly in a medical professional.

It seemed Falstaff had something for his blackmail bag after all.

'About time, too,' he reflected under his breath. Now at least the evening would not be a total loss. And where the devil was Heather? The room ought to have been cleaned up by now...

For that matter, where was everyone? Dick only now noticed just how empty the place looked. He saw no one around, not even the madam. The bar stood vacant. With the exception of the one over-zealous couple round the bend in the hall, he didn't hear anything either.

'*Falstaff*,' growled a voice from behind him.

Dr Falstaff whirled around, startled despite himself. He normally was not prone to such childish reactions of fear, but something about the fellow he now faced served to unnerve him. Not that there was any perceptible reason for it—the man was short and slight enough, even relative to Dick, not to pose any serious physical threat, and his voice, though gravelly, was not exactly disturbing on its own. Yet the doctor could not shake his feeling of uneasiness...

'Do I know you?' he returned, attempting to regain some of his lost composure.

A laugh—a hideous, baleful, menacing laugh—emanated from deep within the newcomer's throat. It was as if he chortled at a private joke, one to which only he possessed the punchline—a joke made, quite possibly, at the doctor's expense. Dick didn't like this at all.

'No, dear doctor,' the stranger said. 'I dare say you don't, not hardly. But I know you. I know you, and that, sir, is what counts here.'

'I don't follow,' Falstaff admitted, rather at a loss for how to deal with the fellow. He'd never seen this man before in his life. How, then, did the bloke know him? And why was he acting so smug, so arrogant, as if he knew something the doctor didn't and were holding it over him in great amusement?

Damn his piercing eyes! thought Dick, surprised—even as the words made their way across his mind—at the intensity with which he felt this hitherto-unknown sentiment. Yet he could not deny the reality: He really, truly did feel the hate, the unrelenting vulnerability, his thought suggested. Why—?

Of course. Of course! he exclaimed in his head. *This fellow*, he realised with a touch of horror that readily transmogrified itself into an intense sinking feeling in the pit of his stomach, *this fellow knows about the will! Good God!* He wasn't certain why he thought this, either, but he swore it felt like the bastard could stare right through him, pierce his heart, his soul, and sound out all the ugly truths inside…

'Oh, you'll follow me in a minute,' the black-haired man said with unsettling surety. His eyes were black, too—or at least so incredibly dark brown that they may as well have been. 'I am giving you a chance,' he said through gritted teeth, as if struggling to rein in intense fury. 'I offer you the most valuable thing in the world to a man.'

'And what's that?' Dick asked, with bravado enough, though he was still unsure where all this was going. 'I have wealth, respect, and intelligence,' he asserted. 'What could you possibly have that I would want?'

'Oh, it is not what I *have* that will interest you,' rejoined the stranger with a sneer. Breaking into a most unfriendly smile, he clarified, 'It is what I hold the power to *take away.*'

'And what is that?' Falstaff asked, unable to meet the man's eyes any longer. (The doctor cursed himself silently for this weakness.) He was afraid to find out the answer...as well he should have been.

'Your life.' The words held all the finality of a death knell.

'What?' sputtered Falstaff in confusion as bafflement and dread warred for supremacy inside him.

'You heard me...*Dick*. The statement is incontrovertible. Do as I say...or *die*. Quite painfully.'

''E'll do it, too,' the madam piped up, popping her head up from behind the bar for a split second. 'Do be careful, doctor!'

'SHUT UP, YOU HAG!' roared the rogue, picking up a lightweight, wooden stand—the one on which Henry'd set his wine glass earlier that night—and hurling it in the madam's general direction. She had already ducked out of sight, but there was a loud crash as it flew into the shelves of the bar. It cracked the mirrored backing and created a cascade of broken bottle-glass.

Falstaff blanched in shock at this display. He had never in his forty-two years seen anything like it.

Who is this man? he thought. *And what has he dragged me into, here?* He had thought he'd be slumming it tonight, not taking his life in his hands!

'Anyone else care to make any clever comments?' the aggressor yelled, looking about the quiet brothel with rage in his eyes, daring anyone to make a move. No one stirred, nor made the slightest peep. 'That's more bloody like it,' he spat, turning his attention back to Dick.

'Wh...what do you want with me?' the doctor asked just above a whisper, shaken and not knowing what to expect.

The scoundrel's only response was an unnerving chuckle.

Dick considered making a run for it. But there was nowhere to go... The newcomer was blocking the end of the hall that led out to the parlour-bar and, beyond that, the door to the outside world. Falstaff knew it would be futile to make a break in the other direction. Because the hallway went round in a sort of rectangular loop, connecting back to itself at precisely the spot where the stranger stood, such an action would've proved downright suicidal.

Dick decided to stall for time, hoping he could get the blighter to back up a bit so he could beat a quick path to the door. He dared not let on that this was his intent, however.

'Madam, get down!' Dr Falstaff shouted suddenly, feigning concern and alarm as he rapidly turned his eyes in the direction of the bar. In reality, the madam was still lying quietly on the floor, protected by the obstructing counter. However, Dick wagered that, as said bar was behind his would-be assailant, the blackguard should have no way of knowing the difference. Once the man became distracted, Falstaff would be able to slip past him and out the door, into the concealing night beyond.

Instead of wheeling around, however, the maniac charged at Falstaff, tackling him into the wall with unexpected ferocity. Dick landed next to Henry's broken glass (which had shattered when the stand went out from under it), groggy from hitting his head on the way down. The interloper loomed over him, leering maliciously as his knee dug into the doctor's chest. The physician found he could not move, his arms and body pinned in such a manner that there was no way for him to lift his centre of gravity.

'Do you think me a fool?!' his attacker bellowed.

'H—how did y—' Falstaff sputtered, unable to comprehend why his sure ruse had failed.

'I. Told. You,' the villain snarled back, digging his nails into the flesh of Dick's arms. 'I know you. And such a selfish bastard as you would *never* stick his neck out to help someone of the...*lower* classes.'

Damn this man and his piercing eyes! Falstaff's brain yelled at him. There they were again, staring right into his soul, and he, Dr Richard Falstaff, a man of wealth, respect, and privilege—in his own opinion, one of the greatest men in London!—was left utterly, hopelessly helpless against them. He hated this man—hated him with a passion and intensity he'd never before known. He wanted to kill him. Desperately.

It shouldn't be that hard, he thought, even as he lay pinioned to the floor. Marking his assailant's height and build, Dick concluded, *He is my lesser physically. If I could but catch him by surprise...* His gaze darted about, looking for a weapon, a distraction, anything.

It settled on the broken glass beside him. Maybe if he could—

'What are you gawking at?' the knave cut Falstaff's thoughts off, replacing Dick's incipient plan with an unwelcome flood of terror.

The doctor's pulse quickened. His heart pounded madly as he saw the rogue's hand reach for the shards. His attacker wore loose, white gloves, coupled with clothes that were too large for his frame. Why, the cape alone nearly swallowed him up! Gentlemen's clothes, these, though this man was a ruffian if ever Dick had seen one. A terrible thought occurred to him: What if this fellow, more than likely a criminal and obviously unbalanced, had pilfered his fine attire from a larger, wealthy victim? What if he had killed the gent and left him lying in the street? It wasn't impossible; in fact (Falstaff now recalled), a man of much propriety had met this fate before. Almost a year ago, he'd been found motionless in the road: an elderly gentleman, well liked and respected, too, a member of the nation's parliament. He had been savagely beaten; his own butler had barely recognised the corpse.

Falstaff shuddered as the thought struck home: He, too, might tonight meet with such an end.

'Get up, you dog!' barked the lowlife, threatening the doctor with a jagged shard of glass. Dick was confused—what was the blighter doing now? Yet he did comply, getting slowly to his feet, careful not to fall into the ready-made weapon at his throat. His assailant slid behind him, holding him hostage all the while. Falstaff could feel the cool of the glass slowly warming from its constant contact with the skin just over his jugular. His throat had gone dry, but he dared not swallow. The sweat from his palms soaked his white gloves through, and he only just retained charge of his functions. He had never felt so humiliated, so *vulnerable*, in his life.

It was about to get worse.

***

From behind the heavy oaken counter, the madam listened. She held death-still lest she disturb the broken glass resting atop her. She knew that if even one chip dropped off and made a sound, *she'd* be the one dealing with the monster in the hall there.

Where was Heather, now? For that matter, where was Henry? She hoped he'd found himself a decent place to hide, lest—

Her thoughts were interrupted by the noise the madman made as he threatened Falstaff and forced him into one of the nearby bedrooms. At least, she remarked silently to herself, it was Dick, not Henry, who was being held hostage. Henry paid well. Dick didn't, if he could avoid it. If she had to lose one of them...

At the sound of the door beginning to creak closed, the madam got up from her makeshift refuge, rising just in time to see the door shut fully. A very final 'click' followed as the lock slid swiftly into place. It was the first room on the right as one entered the hallway—and, she now realised, the very room Heather had gone off to clean...

CHAPTER SEVEN

Falstaff found himself pushed roughly onto the frilly, yellow bedcovers. By the time he realised the shard-knife was no longer at his throat, the ruffian had nearly finished wrapping him in quickly-yanked-off bed-curtains. The doctor struggled to disentangle himself, but that only brought the jagged glass back to his highly vulnerable neck, coupled with a bellicose warning from his captor to lie still or meet death. Given the alternative, Dick complied. He was soon unable to move.

'What in God's name do you want with me?' he cried, fearing for his own survival, painfully aware of his all-too-powerless new position.

'I want you to apologise, you lying dog!' the scoundrel snarled, leaning in uncomfortably close to Falstaff's face, his wavy, black hair rippling from the speed of this swift movement, dark eyes boring into his unhappy captive.

'A—apologise?' Dick stammered, now thoroughly confused. 'Apologise for what? I've never even seen you before in my life!'

'Not to me, you ignoramus!' snapped his assailant, irritated at the doctor's denseness. *But then*, he reminded himself, *he's ignorant of everything I know.* His mind quickly set to work, coming up with just the thing: a plan to cover his tracks and still get what he wanted.

Dick had closed his eyes, not able to withstand the madman's piercing gaze any longer.

'Look at me when I am speaking to you, wretch!' came the harsh command.

Wincing, Falstaff forced his eyes to open. He was frightened, yes, but also a bit miffed. Under the danger lay a sense of...the *indignity* of it all. The entire situation suddenly struck him as most surreal—ludicrous, even. Such things simply *did not happen* to gentlemen of his calibre!

'That's more like it,' growled the reprobate with a nod of satisfaction, noting his unhappy victim's compliance. *He* was in charge, and he intended to keep things that way. He would make Falstaff pay—oh, how he would make him pay! And he knew just the right humiliation for this self-important cad...

'I am going to free you,' he announced, knowing these words would catch the doctor totally off-guard.

'Very good,' managed Falstaff, eyes wide with shock, brows knit in befuddlement.

'*On one condition*,' the brute clarified. His captive waited to hear what. 'You will apologise—'

'To whom?' asked Dick, too quickly.

'DO NOT INTERRUPT ME, CUR!' the fiend howled with fury, grabbing a poker from the fireplace on the other side of the tiny room and bringing it down at full speed.

Falstaff cried out in pain as it struck him cruelly across the belly. The confining curtains wrapped around him proved little help against the force of this rapid blow. The doctor could feel bruises starting to form. He hoped he wasn't bleeding internally.

'Here is how it all will be,' the domineering lowlife now continued, seeing Dick in what he considered a suitable amount of pain for his impertinence. 'You will go to that old hag of a widow, onetime wife of the late Dr Denman. You will bow before her on bended knee and beg her to forgive you. You will explain all the ill you have done the Denman family, from spreading false rumours about Harold to cheating widows and orphans out of their fortune. And you will do it all in a *highly public venue.*'

The thought of taking part in such a spectacle was beyond odious to Dick. Good God, it was the last thing he'd *ever* want to do! (Which was exactly the point.)

'Why in God's name do you care so much about that bloody widow and her snot-nosed little guttersnipe?' spat the doctor, unable to contain himself. His indignation and horror at his proposed fate simply forced the words right out of his mouth. Remembering how his outbursts had previously gone over, he slammed his eyes shut, waiting fearfully for the surely-incoming blow.

None came. Instead, his captor merely gave a feral laugh, then purred at him:

'I don't. In fact, I really rather couldn't care less. They could be run over by a carriage or perish in a horrible fire, for aught I care. Aye, a fire...' He seemed to be thinking to himself, as if pursuing this unplanned mental tangent. From the evil look of pleasure on the man's face, Dick wondered if he were not contemplating setting the blaze himself.

But what, then, is his purpose in demanding that I do as he's proposed? ruminated Dick. *If this whole affair is not about the widow or the Denman name in general...what on earth can it be about?*

As if in answer to the doctor's unvoiced question, the maniac informed him, calmly enough (but with an underlying, gleeful air of malice):

'No, my dear Dr Falstaff. This has nothing to do with them. Not really. It never did.' He smiled unpleasantly.

'I don't understand,' stated Dick, dreading to learn where this might be headed.

'Of course you don't. You're a fool,' the devil condescended, as if it were incontrovertible fact. 'A self-important imbecile so caught up in lauding his own "clever" deeds that he can't see past the nose right on his face, who has no clue of the repercussions his snappish, petty, hateful words can cause.'

Falstaff watched him as he paused, noting that the rogue looked angry, but also a tad... sad? Wistful? Forlorn? He couldn't tell.

Dick cursed inside his head. This was all too strange—damnably, unreally, impossibly strange! Yet he feared to interrupt the man again, and so said nothing.

The scoundrel turned his full attention back to Falstaff without warning, his ire renewed.

'And in case you are wondering,' he snarled out with a sneer, 'just *why* you should cooperate, allow me to enlighten you.' Getting much too close to his face for the doctor's comfort, he went on scornfully, 'If you do not, I assure you, you *will* die. Give me any trouble now, and you perish tonight. Renege on our arrangement later, and I shall find you then. And do not think your wealth or name can save you. I know better. Wherever you are, I swear to God and Satan I will track you down at last. So, your punishment is really up to you. But I know you are a coward. I know the choice you'll make.

'With that in mind, we must now set to work. You shall recite to me, verbatim, exactly what you plan to tell the widow. All of it.' His look brooked no disagreement.

Left with no other choice, Falstaff yammered on and on, not only admitting that he'd started the rumours about his cousin, but confessing things that even his assailant had not known. The matter of the will, for instance: Harold Denman had actually drawn up a version wherein everything passed indirectly to Madge and Ginny, thanks to a very trustworthy young lawyer friend of the family. Falstaff admitted that he had chanced upon this document while visiting for a family dinner. Before Harold had had the opportunity to show it to his lawyer, Dick had filched it from his 'uncle's' study and, in his own words, 'disposed of it', knowing full well the outcome this would cause.

Only one portion of Falstaff's narrative did his dark-haired captor deem too lacking in detail: Dick's role in spreading rumours about Dr Denman and his purported deviant proclivities. Granted, Falstaff had admitted he'd begun them, but he'd omitted one small but crucial fact: that he'd *invented* these accusations, contriving them from nothing so as to ruin the unsuspecting Denman by these awful and unseemly lies.

'But—' protested Falstaff.

'"But" what, you selfish little whelp?' the madman roared, giving the helpless doctor a fresh wave of fright. Raising the fireplace poker threateningly above his head, he shouted, 'You will tell the truth or meet your death right now, I swear to God!'

Dick shut his eyes in fear, his every muscle tensing lest the vile brute beat him dead. Mewling pitiably, he sputtered, 'But I *am* telling all the truth, I swear to you, I swear! I didn't make up any of it! Uncle Harry *was* a homosexual!'

'LIES!' accused the villain, setting out to bring the iron rod down with force.

'He did such things with *me*!' cried Dick, tears streaming, for the first time, down his face. 'Oh God, oh please, don't kill me!' he begged, eyes closed, awaiting the first strike of many that would come now, he was sure, to rain upon him and send him to his grave.

Instead, he heard a loud and heavy clang. Startled, he instinctively looked for what had caused the sound. The iron poker lay on the floor, the maniac apparently having dropped it without meaning to. Then Dick chanced to settle his tear-blurred gaze upon his deranged attacker, and was absolutely shocked at what he beheld: The knave still stood there, in the exact position as before save that he now seemed somehow...*different.* His demeanour had shifted, Dick thought, though in a way he could not easily place. The hand that had held the heavy implement of terror had gone slack, though it was still kept aloft by an arm seemingly frozen in place. A dull look of horror radiated out the ruffian's eyes, and now his arm fell limply by his side. Falstaff thought the man more shocked than even he was, if that were possible.

Without any warning, his former assailant quickly and inexplicably made a beeline for the door, throwing back the lock and slipping out of the room almost before the doctor realised what was happening.

The madam heard frantic footsteps racing down the hall, then running past the barstools and the lounge, heading away, away, more rapidly than she would've thought possible. Within a matter of seconds, their owner had fled out the door, disappearing into the night beyond.

'Don't just stand there, Laura!' yelled the madam to the dumbfounded girl, who'd ventured to peek out of her room. 'Move your arse and bar the door! Right quick!'

Laura did as she was told, sliding the bolt solidly into place. A collective sigh of relief then issued from all within the bordello.

''E's gone, thank God,' observed the other twin, Lauren, stepping out from behind a red drape.

'Aye,' agreed the madam, sitting herself down upon a stool. 'I 'ope 'e didn't 'urt no one tonight—or kill 'em. Lord knows we can't afford to 'ave the coppers come snoopin' 'round 'ere.'

Slowly, things began to grow more normal. The madam dispatched Lauren and Jeanine to clean up the ruined bar, while she herself untied the shaken Falstaff. He quickly returned to his typical, haughty demeanour (for the most part, anyway), indignantly informing the madam, in no uncertain terms, that she'd never find him in this shady establishment again, and that if she didn't quit making a fuss in trying to convince him otherwise, the police would shut her down for sure, he'd see to that! She relented, and he took his leave, hailing a passing hansom and escaping to the 'safer' side of town.

Sometime after this, Heather quietly let herself out of the wardrobe wherein she'd hidden this entire time. She had heard everything. Relieved not to have been found, she let out a tremendous sigh, then collapsed gratefully onto the soft and frilly, sunshine-yellow bedcovers.

CHAPTER EIGHT

Henry, too, had not met with his end—though, to be honest, he had feared that fate. Instead, he returned to his fine, large home, simultaneously shaken to his core and grateful for his life, given all that had transpired tonight. He found himself distressingly unsure of what to do. He'd thought he'd been released from those damned fits of his, but his unproductive talk with Dr Falstaff had proved otherwise. And he'd had another on his way home. He'd ducked into the nearest blind alleyway he could find, shaking and sweating and praying no one saw him as he'd writhed about on the cold, hard ground in the painful throes of his affliction. Tonight had been a wash—far worse than a wash, in fact. Everything had gone downhill from the moment he'd tried to convince Dick Falstaff to act like a decent human being. Well, one thing was certain: He'd never go into that brothel again.

Not even to see Jeanine? his mind wondered to him, even as he thought he'd made the promise.

'No. No,' he muttered quietly to himself, shaking his head slightly as he did. 'I can't.' He continued, mentally, *It would be too risky. Supposing Falstaff were to show himself again? I can't afford it.* For Dick put the doctor's own wellbeing in jeopardy.

I cannot chance the risk of any further fits, thought Harry, as he prepared for bed. *God forbid, one might take place in public.* He prayed no more occurred at all, but knew it would be ever so much worse in front of witnesses. It had been by only the slimmest of margins that he'd managed to evade that happening tonight.

I will avoid the man entirely, he planned. *Nowhere will I go that he might be.* He knew this could prove difficult, seeing as the social circles within which they moved were known to overlap, but he resolved, *I will do what I must, even if it should appear a trifle odd to my acquaintances.*

And thus it was. Any parties Falstaff attended, Henry made sure to absent. When he hosted some himself, he never put Falstaff on the guest list—not that he ever had previously.

He did tell John about his episode in the brothel, not wanting to keep secrets from his loyal friend. (He'd made *that* mistake the first time around.) And here, he thought, was someone—perhaps the only man alive—who could understand his strange predicament. But John was not receptive to his story. He thought Harry'd got into those damned drugs of his again, that he'd reopened his peculiar lab and had hallucinated the whole incident. When Henry protested, he was met with John's assertion that, although it all must have *seemed* quite real, many substances were capable of causing such delusions, and that the doctor would do well to heed his warnings. John's intent and line of reasoning were infallible—there was no question there—but, Harry realised, it was now apparent that his old chum had never believed *any* of the most extraordinary things Henry had told him—not even on the morning when he'd come to John after finding himself in the morgue.

How could I have been so blind and stupid? Henry berated himself silently, wondering why he hadn't seen the truth. *Of course John wouldn't find my words believable—at least, not about something so fantastic. He is a rational man—not narrow-minded like poor Hastie but, still, logical almost to a fault. And, I do suppose, had I myself not known all that I do, it might have seemed a lie to me as well. It's certainly unreal enough as is.*

He decided to let the matter drop. It wasn't worth ruining a friendship over. Though he had so hoped to have John to confide in regarding this dreadful problem of his...

For John's part, he put Harry's tale down to too many drugs, and his contact with said drugs down to personal idiosyncrasy. Some men were alcoholics, some cheated on their wives, some hoarded money all their lives and never once enjoyed it. He would do his best to keep the doctor on the straight and narrow path, but he also knew that Henry was his own person and thus could not be cured of his unhealthful habits solely by the will or intent of a well-meaning friend.

At least he isn't an opium-sot, the lawyer consoled himself.

***

Some time passed—several weeks, in fact—and things appeared to settle down to normal. Henry had no more of his fits (or drug-taking, as John preferred to call it). Dick made an even greater arse of himself than usual, this behaviour perhaps arising as a manifestation of his happiness at not having been slain. And, predictably enough, he forewent admitting any wrongdoing, his personal confession not forthcoming, feeling, as he did, quite safe among the company of his peers. He didn't run into Henry, a fact he rather regretted, seeing as he could hold over him the knowledge of the elder doctor's epileptic episode. For that was what Falstaff knew he had witnessed the beginnings of; the signs were unmistakeable.

This information, the younger man concluded, *might very well be worthy of blackmail. Not for too much, I suppose—certainly not the way addiction or homosexuality could be used to ensnare him—but it is useful knowledge nonetheless. A doctor, prone to epilepsy! What weakness, and what fraud!*

Only one other happening worthy of mention occurred in this time. A few days after the terrible confrontation, a mysterious, unmarked package arrived at the bordello. Upon opening it, the madam discovered a tidy sum, just sitting there, in cash—more than enough to pay for the damages her whorehouse had sustained. She found the whole affair most curious.

'You're damned right I'm suspicious,' she began, addressing all her girls, 'but money's money, loves. Be glad it don't come out of all your earnin's.'

CHAPTER NINE

Some months passed, and summer turned to autumn, finding Henry in a thoroughly pensive frame of mind. The season no doubt held partial responsibility for this, as chilly eves and vibrant, dying foliage could turn the thoughts of all but self-important dullards inward. In this reflective vein, Henry sat inside the old Denman manor, thinking. A cheery fire glowed soothingly before him, its warmth denying the night's unkind chill. The fabric of the nail-head chair felt soft and warm against the doctor's skin, the kind of comfort arising only from a piece of lasting quality, made with fine materials and even finer craftsmanship, then lovingly worn in. This particular specimen was a genuine Louis XV, having come furnished with the house when Henry'd purchased it from Dr Denman.

Henry now found himself in a distasteful quandary regarding his past mentor. He had a source—the identity of whom he had no desire to expose, lest his own name be ruined by association—through whom he had recently learned of the shameful practices Harold had done with (or was it 'to'?) his younger cousin, Richard Falstaff. This, from a man Henry had so admired and defended! Yet he knew—remembered—the kindness, the nobility that had been Denman's hallmark, knew, if ever he knew anything, the genuineness of it, the personal integrity...

Integrity. That chord struck home. Had Harold really been the man he'd thought? Everything seemed to come into question, now. Was he, Henry, truly who he thought himself to be? Deep down, as at the bottom of a stony well, at his very inner core...what lay there? Who was he, really? In his mind's eye, he beheld his face as if mirrored in a dark reflecting pool. He wondered if it were his real face after all. This visage that he called his own... If character were evidenced in body—well, what then?

What is my true appearance? Henry pondered, fearing in his soul what the reality might be. And, because he feared that it were so, almost immediately, the image in his mind began to alter, twisting inexorably into something horrific and abhorrent to the doctor, a face that frightened and disturbed him to the depths of his being.

'God forbid that I am truly—' he half-cried, unable to bring himself to finish the words aloud.

A knock sounded sharply at the thick door to his chambers.

'Yes?' called the physician, caught unprepared for this sudden intrusion but grateful for it all the same.

'Sorry to disturb you, sir. May I come in?' asked the butler from the other side of the door.

'Yes, of course,' replied Henry, having been so preoccupied with his own inner, mental distractions that he'd forgotten to ask the man in.

The door opened, and in came the butler, bearing an envelope on a silver, filigree-etched tray.

'A message for you,' the servant announced, 'recently delivered. It appears to be from Mr Cedric Crespin.'

'Indeed?' remarked the doctor, curious as to what Cedric could have sent him. He hadn't seen the chap since the masked ball at the latter's home, over a year and a half ago. He wondered what business the wealthy banker might have with him now.

'Do you wish me to open it for you, sir?' the butler queried, still holding the tray as he stood awaiting his master's response.

'No, thank you. Just set it on the desk there. I shall peruse it later.'

'Very good, sir. Is there anything more you may require?'

'No, nothing else tonight, I think. That will be all.'

'Very good. Goodnight, sir,' the butler intoned, bowing with respect as he stepped out.

'Goodnight,' Henry replied, waiting till the heavy door clicked shut and the servant's measured, unobtrusive footfall retreated down the hall.

Opening the envelope, the doctor discovered an invitation to Mr and Mrs

Crespin's annual Christmas party, which Henry had not attended these two years past. Also enclosed was a personal note from Cedric himself, somewhat telegraphic in style (as was the man's wont), but warm enough despite this. The body read as follows:

> Sorry to learn of this past year's troubles. Glad to hear you're back to your old self again. Do let's see each other soon. My yearly Christmas get-together will take place before long; you'll find the invite enclosed. I do look forward to catching up with you there. Please send a message within three weeks' time to let us know whether you plan to attend. Looking forward to seeing you.
>
> All the best,
> Mr Cedric Crespin
>
> P.S.: Mattie and Alex hope you'll come as well.

Well, thought Henry, *what a lovely surprise.* He hadn't seen Cedric in what seemed like ages and, in truth, had feared the jolly banker had decided to have nothing to do with him. The doctor's illness had previously forced him to remove himself from the limelight of any and all social affairs, lest he suffer an attack while in public, and he had been so preoccupied with trying to find a cure for his condition that he'd answered hardly any of the letters received during that time, even the ones from his friends. It had been a most horrible, slowly maddening isolation. He was quite relieved to be done with it...he hoped. He had not undergone a relapse or regression of any kind these past few months (having been assiduously careful to avoid that horrid Falstaff—the man just set him off, somehow), and this gave Henry hope.

Another bright point in receiving this recent invitation was that Cedric loathed Dick Falstaff nearly as much as did the good doctor. Oh, Crespin could be civil enough around Falstaff, but any who read nuances could tell, judging by the way they spoke, that no love was lost between them. They were each too coolly, formally polite—though Dick often seemed to enjoy his attempts at rattling Cedric. At any rate, for Henry, the happy thing about this upcoming party was that he knew Falstaff would not be invited. That alone made cause for celebration.

***

The doctor sent his answer the next day, by early post, eagerly anticipating the merry time ahead. His happiness shone through upon his face, his features bright, his brow no longer furrowed, the green of his eyes seeming somehow more intense. Or perhaps it was just his smile, which he, out of habit, tried to hide as best he could (in an effort to appear more serious and respectable, lest any think him subject to frivolity), though to no avail. He silenced his preoccupations, or at least distanced them into subtle, muted tones of vague anxiety that could be heard but faintly amidst the all-enveloping clarion of his fresh contentedness. All around, the leaves were dying, but inside, he felt alive. He perused the falling foliage not with sadness but with joy: This was as it should be; he bore witness to the magnificence of nature's change in action. At this express moment, the chaotic flow of leaves bespoke the very order of all things: casting off the old to make way for the new, one season in the midst of morphing into the next, one step of the ever-renewing cycle gradually and beautifully giving way to that which followed, and Man, plants, animals—the world!—a part of it all. In the falling of a leaf, this man saw God.

CHAPTER TEN

The day of Cedric's party soon arrived, and found Henry on the Crespins' doorstep, gift in hand. One servant admitted him; another announced him as he came in.

Cedric's was a magnificent place, built in the early 1800s, and the scene that now greeted Harry's eyes made it all the richer still: The foyer was festooned with garlands, two rounded, earthy ribbons of pine green, contrasting with thick panelling of their native wood, against which they rested. These twin natural streamers of winsome evergreen, arranged in perfect symmetry, allowed the eye of whosoever viewed them to follow down these lines, without the slightest effort of the mind. The garlands terminated where the foyer did and, at this point, one's gaze shifted as well. For here, just at the threshold of the house's largest room, a most impressive vision made itself known.

In the centre of the room stood a massive Christmas tree (perhaps the largest Henry'd ever seen), fresh and green and bedecked with all sorts of wonderful, sparkling ornaments—glass, porcelain, painted wood, shine-sided paper—in an array of marvellous colours, sizes, and shapes. Atop the magnificent evergreen's apex perched a Christmas angel, clad in pure white robes, its soft, diaphanous wings and golden halo glittering.

A dark, oaken table, tastefully laid out and lavishly laden with a smorgasbord of sundry, sumptuous foodstuffs, stood to the right of the tree. On the left side of the room, a cherry staircase, flush against the dark-panelled wall, led up, then turned right, providing the back wall with a full-length balcony, from which a few of the partygoers observed the goings-on below. In the main, open space before the giant evergreen, couples danced back and forth while hired musicians played. It was, all in all, a marvellous, festive scene.

Henry wandered about, seeing several familiar faces spin by him on the dance floor, and noticed a couple of acquaintances at the buffet. Yet he did not spy the host of the soiree. Where was Cedric, Henry wondered, and did he know the doctor had arrived?

Henry made his way about the room, more slowly than he would have liked. Many of the upper crust (and *nouveau riche*) had not yet had the chance to speak to the good doctor one on one, at least not since his horrible ordeal. Though they feigned concern, they were terribly curious and their suspicion was only thinly cloaked. The truth was that they loved a freak show. The mysterious, the bizarre, the unanticipated—all of these described Henry's all-too-publicised travail. How had he escaped the clutches of that madman? Had he feared for his life? Had the villain threatened him with bodily harm?

Was it true, what the papers said: Had Henry really been just unlucky enough to be picked by a maniac by pure chance, for ransom's sake? (Some of the guests meant here to fish for more, implying as they did that the respected doctor might have had something to hide, and blackmail thusly might have been involved. Yet never did they ever *say* as much.) Henry gave them the same statement he and John had worked up for the papers and never deviated one iota from the tale. Eventually, the gossipmongers realised they would get no more from him, aside from unrelated (if polite) conversation. Thankfully, they drifted away then, leaving him to try to get back his now-exhausted peace of mind. The doctor at last drew in a deep breath—his breathing had gone shallow, thanks to the recent barrage of queries—then let it out in a relieved sigh.

'Henry.' The voice came from behind him, from the space between the tree and the rear wall. It sounded more a statement than a greeting, as if the utterer cared not for the name's bearer, save for what he could someway exploit.

Henry turned. There, standing exactly where he had imagined based on the origin of the voice, was Dr Richard Falstaff.

'Dick,' the elder physician returned in disbelief, wondering why on earth this man was here. The barest tinge of nausea laced its way through him, starting in his stomach and growing inexplicably more acute as it traversed his chest and throat. He did not like this man. Nothing good ever came of encountering him. Harry wondered what he wanted with him now. 'How have you been?' the surprised doctor managed. In truth, he really didn't care to hear the answer and, deep down, half-heartedly wished this man would die, if only so he wouldn't have to deal with him at all. And yet he hated himself for feeling this way, for though Falstaff was a cad, he had his reasons, and death ought not be wished on anyone.

'Well enough,' the decade-younger man rejoined. Henry could see in his eyes he was up to something. 'But what of you?' His tone turned conspiratorial, quieter, somewhat threatening. 'Have you been well, too? Or have you had any more of your...shall we say...*episodes*?'

A chill rush of horror swept through Henry's veins like ice. His face went pale, his legs felt suddenly weak.

He knows, he thought, shock and panic fighting for supremacy inside him. *He knows my secret. No! This must not be! Have I really come all this way, so very far, just to have it all crash down around me? And by so mean and inconsequential a man? And how did he find out? Oh, God, he's the* worst *person who could have learned of it! Oh, God!*

Yet Henry managed a courteous, if somewhat shaken, 'Wh...whatever do you mean?' It was a stalling statement, nothing more, but it proved the most he could muster at the moment.

Falstaff rolled his eyes. 'Come off it, man,' he admonished, annoyed. 'I know what I saw when you left that night. I'm a physician, too, you know. And unlike a lot of people, apparently, *I* can put two and two together.'

Henry, looking nervous as a doe before a deerhound, asked hurriedly, 'Do you think we might discuss this somewhere else?' He glanced about. 'Perhaps upstairs, in one of Crespin's rooms, with a door as barrier to any prying ears?'

'Certainly,' Dick readily agreed, a look of glee and haughtiness spreading across his face. This was perfect blackmail material after all! It had taken him long enough to find the doctor—almost as if Henry'd been avoiding him, he thought—but now his day had finally arrived. This was going to end terribly well, he just knew it! 'Well then, go upstairs,' Falstaff instructed. 'The second door you come across, go in. I shall make my way there in a moment.'

Henry did as he was bidden, trying his level best not to be noticed. Luckily, the few persons who'd before stood along the balcony had, by this time, gone downstairs to get some food. He slipped in surreptitiously, with no one there the wiser. Dick followed shortly after.

The room looked to be Cedric's study—or library, if the man didn't read overmuch—and Falstaff found Henry seated in a soft, brownleathered chair. The elder man had felt he'd needed to sit down, after what Dick had said. He'd tried to calm himself, regaining some of his composure, though by no means all.

If that wretched Falstaff knows my secret, he had thought, *there is but one thing in my favour: I know his. I would disgrace the memory of Denman even further, should I tell it, but, God willing, such shall not come to pass.* This was his only hope of protection against Falstaff, whom Henry knew to exploit and blackmail whomever he could with whatever he could until they had nothing left to give. And then, after all that, Dick would *expose* them, just as he had done with Harold Denman.

Bearing such weighty matters well in mind, Henry warily marked the entrance of Dr Falstaff. The latter wore a look of self-importance and such smugness that the elder doctor had to do his best to contain a wave of alarm that threatened to rise up and pull him down. Although he did succeed in this endeavour, clearly, some of his worry had slipped through: Dick's confidence now seemed bolstered severalfold, while Henry hated being here at all. And so it was with much aplomb that Falstaff found himself a seat and pulled it up across from Henry's chair, deliciously aware of the anxiety his new proximity would cause the all-too-nervous elder man.

'Now that we both are here,' Falstaff began, 'there is something we simply must discuss.'

He smirked in self-approval. 'It seems, my most esteemed of fellow doctors, that you have something which you tried to hide: a shortcoming, a moral–body weakness, a failing that shall prove you quite the fraud and be a spot upon your cherished name.'

Henry, in a restive state already, now found his worst suspicions well confirmed.

He knows, the unhappy doctor realised. *I prayed this day would never come to pass, and certainly not with this man the one who found me out.* He grimaced inwardly and almost sobbed. Yet still Henry did not betray his mind, would not give Dick the satisfaction of seeing all the turmoil he'd caused. He knew Falstaff viewed him now as easy prey.

Henry pulled himself together, querying the scoundrel thus, 'What price, then, I ask, do you seek from me? What would you exact, thanks to my misfortune? And what harm will you perpetrate against me should I deem your proposal's price too dear?'

Dick named a most exorbitant amount (more, indeed, than the doctor's considerable fortune), which he knew Henry would never agree to pay.

'Or,' Falstaff added, as if he did the doctor a great favour simply by offering, 'I could be persuaded to take a portion of the old Denman manor instead.'

This, of course, meant part of Henry's— formerly Dr Denman's—house, which Henry most certainly did *not* want cut into flats. To break up the old building would not only ruin its splendour, it would also desecrate the memory of his mentor. (Not to mention that he knew Dick likely wouldn't stop at just *one* piece of the structure...) Henry still held a fondness for the late man's memory, despite the complication brought to his attention recently. In fact, he reflected, it was this new knowledge that would save his hide in his current, lamentable situation.

'You are right, naturally,' he told Dr Falstaff, 'in thinking I do not wish my shameful secret revealed.'

Dick's eyes lit up in a most self-applauding fashion as he anticipated completing his revenge against his 'uncle'. He silently congratulated himself on how easy it had been to get one of Harold's old students to crack.

'However,' Henry continued, his tone changing, certain now, 'I doubt you want the world to know yours, either.' He looked Dick straight in the eye, letting the implications sink in.

Falstaff felt confusion snap sharply around his mind, paired with a small but potent shot of panic. These were succeeded almost immediately by doubt—for how could anyone know his secret?—but though these two unpleasant feelings became muted, they still would not subside.

'What are you talking about?' Dick snapped, self-righteous as ever.

'I am referring,' Henry clarified, though it pained him as he did so, 'to the most...

unseemly—even *criminal*—relationship you shared with your late "uncle".'

Dick blanched, shocked, then reddened with fury and embarrassment. It took him a few moments to find words to respond to this most unanticipated revelation: Henry *knew*.

'*How?!*' Falstaff blurted out loud, clenching his fists as a wave of anger took him. He'd never been so galled in all his life! He had been so sure he'd had the elder doctor over a barrel... How on earth had his intended victim found him out?!

Now it was Henry's turn to be confused.

'What do you mean, "how"?' he queried Falstaff, unthinkingly. He wasn't sure where all this stood, now. His confusion only added to his anxiety.

'What do you mean, "what do I mean, 'how'"?! Are you stupid? "How" means "how", as in, "How the devil did you learn about my—my...my uncle?!"' he exclaimed, exasperated at the doctor's pretending to be dense.

Suddenly, the realisation snapped into Falstaff's mind that Henry was probably responding this way intentionally, playing him, in an attempt to keep him off-balance and cloud his mind with emotions, thus ensuring Dick would wind up in a less-than-advantageous position during the impending blackmail negotiations.

Ah, so that's his game, deduced Dick with a twinge of self-applause. *Well then, I shan't fall for this low ruse.* Instead, he made up his mind to calm himself (as best he could), to approach this unforeseen dilemma from a more rational perspective, keeping in mind what he knew to be embarrassing to Henry—epilepsy—and how to seek to stem the damage his own past avuncular misdeeds might wreak.

'Well, I don't give a damn how you learned what happened,' Falstaff snapped. 'Your epilepsy is not the only shameful secret I've unearthed about you.' He was lying—bluffing, really—assuming that Henry, like most men of his social calibre, had secrets he would rather remained kept. Dick had no clue precisely what these were, in Henry's case, but gambled that he had them nonetheless.

Henry, for his part, could not be absolutely sure that Falstaff did not know what he now claimed, but wagered the forty-something doctor hadn't discovered his biggest secret, else he would've mentioned it already. Additionally, Henry was shocked as it dawned on him that the only thing Falstaff had deduced about his troubles was that he suffered from attacks of epilepsy. Well, this was jolly grand! A wave of relief washed over him, and he queried Falstaff bemusedly:

'To what are you referring? And how did you surmise I suffered seizures?'

Dick truly had no reply for the first of Henry's enquiries (seeing as it had all been a ruse), so he ignored it, buying himself time by answering the second question first.

'Well, anyone of intelligence with any medical training whatsoever could have told from the rather obvious symptoms you presented—shortly before running out of the room that night—that you were about to enter into an epileptic fit: dilated pupils, agitation, a look of mild hysteria coupled with apparent and sudden disorientation. Why, it's a wonder none of our colleagues have yet figured out the truth. They're rather less intelligent than I gave them credit for,' he concluded, adding, just for good measure, 'Sightless fools, the lot of them.'

'Indeed,' observed Henry in response to Dick's method of diagnosis. 'I should have supposed you'd see through me.'

'But you didn't,' countered Falstaff, tacking on the obvious insult. 'Though I'm really not surprised.'

'I see,' said Henry, purposefully choosing not to respond verbally to the jab at his intelligence.

'Yet now I must ask *you*,' Dick asserted, reddening at the ears as he recalled that someone knew his deeds, 'where *did* you chance to learn of my...relations...with that hypocrite of whom you were so fond?'

'Denman?' Henry echoed.

Dick merely rolled his eyes, as if to say 'of course, you twit.'

'I have my sources,' came Henry's pat answer.

'Yes, I'm sure you do,' Falstaff rejoined. 'As does everyone. Don't be so vague.' He was more than a bit ticked off at this hemming and hawing, for it ate him alive that someone had found him out. He *had* to know how such had happened, and squelch the source. Then maybe he could quiet Henry, too. But first he had to unearth who it was, a fact that only Henry seemed to know. And the senior physician was proving infuriatingly, intentionally evasive.

'I'd rather his identity stay secret,' the elder man asserted. He added, with just a wisp of anger and the barest slip of a sneer, 'You, of all people, should know the importance of keeping one's blackmail sources private. Blackguards always do.'

'Then what does that make you, my fellow doctor? It's obvious you've never won debates where any trace of logic was involved. Don't bother to insult your intellectual superiors; you will always lose, as you just have.'

'Better to lose a debate and not one's good name than the reverse, *Dick*,' countered Henry, wishing this whole talk would just end soon. So he had gotten a little flustered and there had been a small hole in his logic. Was that any reason to crucify him, as Falstaff did?

Well, the elder doctor concluded to himself, *it really doesn't matter, for this man is not worth any trouble on my part. He huffs and bluffs and insults left and right, but I am safe from him. He cannot harm me with his slander as he did Denman—or, rather,* it occurred to him, *with the truth, in Harold's case. God, I'm still having trouble trying to wrap my thoughts around that...*

He stood up suddenly, wanting to leave this otherwise cosy room, which Falstaff ruined by his mere presence.

'If you will excuse me,' Henry said, addressing his would-have-been blackmailer. 'I believe our conversation is at an end, Dr Falstaff. If you have nothing more to say, I shall take my leave. There's a party with at least a few decent folk in attendance taking place downstairs and, truth be told, I would much rather go down there with them than stay up here with you.' He gave Dick a nasty look, briefly wondering at his own uncivil words. It seemed this fellow just brought out the worst in him…

'Oh, don't be such a woman, Henry,' Dick shot back, the latest in a series of barbs he'd levelled at the doctor just tonight. He rose from his chair. Gesturing toward the door, he announced sourly, 'I certainly don't want to keep you.'

'Good,' declared Henry, turning immediately and walking toward the door. He exited without so much as a goodbye. He knew this was the height of rudeness, but simply couldn't bring himself to acknowledge Falstaff with the proper social respect. *Not that he deserves any, but still…* He was more disappointed with his own ungentlemanly conduct during their exchange than angry at the regular barrage of put-downs Dick had shot his way. After all, he, Henry, had been in the more favourable position; the secret he'd learned about Dick and his so-called uncle had made Falstaff's accusations of epilepsy pale in comparison. Why, then, had he so easily given in to his lesser nature and insulted the blighter back?

He decided to get back to the party. Ruminating on Falstaff would get him nowhere. The man was never going to change, and he, Henry, acted worse simply from being around him.

Where is Cedric? he then wondered. *After all, it is his party, yet I've not seen him once this night.* He was also privately curious as to why the banker had deigned to invite Falstaff here at all. Yet, despite all the unpleasantries Henry had just endured, he did find a kind of reassurance in at last knowing where he stood with Falstaff. The fact that Henry had the upper hand (for once!) didn't hurt matters, either.

Making his way down the stairs, he chanced to spy the host of the soiree. Cedric stood amongst a sea of faces, a human tide of suits and evening gowns. Henry hastened toward him, nearly as happy to see a friendly face as he was to be rid of Falstaff's trying company.

'Henry, old boy!' Cedric greeted him, spotting the doctor dodging through the crowd. 'Fancy running into you tonight!' he joked good-naturedly, moving in the direction of his guest. 'It has been *ages*!' he exclaimed as they finally met, grabbing Henry's hand in a jovial shake. 'How *have* you been? Why, I'll bet I've not laid eyes on you at least these two years past! But you seem to have recovered well enough, from the look of you. Jolly good, that, I do declare! Mattie, Alex, do come join us!' he encouraged, looking over his shoulder toward his wife and son. Facing Henry once more, he explained, 'I've been eager for Alex to meet with you, you know. The boy could learn a lot, or perhaps just draw some inspiration, from you.'

Henry regarded his host quizzically. What was Cedric on about? And how was he, Henry, such an 'inspiration'? He felt odd about someone using that term to refer to him—a bit guilty, in fact—for what would everyone think of him if they knew the truth? He imagined 'inspiration' would *not* be among the epithets...

Matilda ('Mattie') and Alexander ('Alex') caught up to Cedric, who reacquainted them with the doctor. They exchanged greetings and, in the course of the conversation, it became clear what Crespin had meant about his son getting to know Henry better: The boy wanted to become a doctor.

'Or at least that's what it is this week, hey, Alex?' Cedric ribbed good-humouredly.

'I mean it this time,' the child informed his father. 'I really do want to be a doctor.' He turned to Henry. 'Like you, sir.'

Henry could see seriousness in the lad's face—unusual, for one so young (Alex was, by the look of him, only ten or eleven years old). Henry himself hadn't known what he'd wanted for his own profession until much later on in life. He'd tried his hand at a great many things—respectable, intellectual, purposeful pursuits—but medicine, for him, had at last won out. He'd valued its capacity to do good, to salve those who were suffering or even turn back death. Not every case was a success, of course, and it weighed on him that not all could be saved. So he had turned his attention to medicine's *potential*, having plumbed the limits of its practical design. Techniques, as they stood, could go only so far and no further. This had offended him in its own way, for why should mankind be condemned to suffer when, surely, somewhere, some method existed for bettering the earthly stay of Man, some idea just waiting to be realised by the mind...

And yet, where had it led him? Granted, he'd been waylaid by his own distractions and had pursued a particular line of experimentation for less than honourable reasons in the end, but his original intent had not been bad—quite the contrary.

The boy's admiration for him made the doctor feel uneasy. It wasn't just the sense of his own unworthiness, or the battle this most penitent of feelings did with his all-too-flattered pride. No, this was something more and went much deeper. He felt a sense of internal dis-ease, almost physical in nature, as if, inside, his heart had taken ill when he remembered his hypocrisy.

But, of course, he dared not even hint at this, as far as any others were concerned.

No, I must appear quite normal; I must set my mind at ease, or at least must seem that way to everyone. He hated these charades but had to play them nonetheless. In this respect, he differed none too much from most of his peers.

And so it was that Henry appeared quite at ease as he conversed with Alex. The boy desired to help people, in earnest. He was also positively fascinated with the organic, machine-like inner workings that kept the human body on its course: how the heart pumped blood to every tiny artery, how the stomach knew to digest food, how a broken bone could mend itself. A 'marvellous machine, designed by God and Nature', as Alex put it.

That was very true, Henry reflected. Oh, how he wished he had been satisfied! To marvel at Nature and God's human symmetry, to look upon Creation and say 'Good!' instead of mourning what He had neglected...

This boy, Alex, was happy with his condition and, apparently, the world. In such, he was leagues ahead of Henry.

Or, the man of medicine reflected, *he may be leagues behind; I do not know. He still has dreams and hopes, as yet untarnished. I pray he may fare better than I have. If not...* In his mind's eye, the doctor saw a possible future of the boy's, a cruel encapsulation of life's sorrows: the loss of innocence and of one's parents; the weight of years; the deaths of those one tried so hard to save, not only on the operating table; opportunities lost; friendships gone sour; words left unsaid, or said that should never have been; the loss of hope; the perversion of dreams; the ruck and run of days, down into despair... He prayed life would not do to this young lad what it had done to him. And he, Henry, was one of the lucky ones: He was not dead or seriously ill, he had a fine home, servants, wealth, good food, at least a few close friends, a panoply of books to read by the fire, and one of the finest names in all of London. Perhaps, he thought, he should've been happy. Yet he wanted his life to be something more than long. Where was the *meaning*?

Well, perchance he could at least help this bright boy. After Mattie had taken young Alex on to bed (for, in truth, it had grown rather late), Henry offered Cedric his assistance in anything the banker's son might need, as far as learning medicine required. He would, he said, be willing even to be the boy's mentor—if Mr Crespin deemed it fit, of course.

'Why, that's jolly good of you, Henry, jolly good! You needn't ask for my permission there!' Cedric exclaimed in a crisp, merry tone.

Henry nodded, and smiled at the elation of his friend. Crespin's ebullient nature could take some getting used to, but he liked this lively man. He found his animated spirits... well, rather refreshing, actually. This was quite possibly the most straightforward, honest, open, convivial gent the doctor had encountered in his life. In his mind, he placed him as the absolute antithesis of Dick Falstaff. Which brought him to the question:

'If you don't mind my asking, Cedric, why—that is to say, I have been wondering—I suppose you've seen Dr Falstaff here tonight?'

Crespin nodded. 'He flagged me down when he first arrived. Pissant of a man,' the banker declared. 'Why do you ask?'

Now Henry was thoroughly confused. Hadn't this party been by invitation only? If Cedric didn't like Falstaff, then why was Dick here?

'Well, it's not any of my business, really, but since I had run into him—'

'Oh, did you?' Crespin interjected. 'Terribly sorry.' A look of genuine sympathy crossed his face.

'Yes, it wasn't exactly enjoyable,' Henry commiserated. 'But the encounter set me wondering...'

'...what Falstaff was doing here?' Cedric surmised.

'Precisely.' Henry nodded.

'Ah. I do apologise for that. My aunt Mildred's visiting from out of town.'

Henry looked at him, not quite following.

His host elaborated, 'Aunt Millie is quite a fan of Falstaff's—though, for the life of me, I cannot fathom why—and as she doesn't see us all that often and has been getting on in years... Sometimes, sacrifices must be made.' He raised an eyebrow, a mischievous look in his eye. 'Besides, she's leaving tomorrow.

And I don't plan to have Dick Falstaff back ever again if I can help it.'

'Ah,' Henry said as it all became clear to him. 'Well, I must say, I am relieved to know that's so.' He shuddered as he thought of Dick again. 'That fellow is by far the most disagreeable man I've ever had the misfortune to have met.'

'Be sure you don't pull any punches, Henry,' Cedric ribbed him. 'Though, to be frank, I'm glad we see eye to eye on the matter. It amazes me how easily he fools people.'

'Only for the first ten minutes,' Harry contended. 'Then one begins to see past his façade.'

'Five,' countered Crespin, holding up his open hand.

'Three, if one's discerning,' shot back Henry with a smile.

'Two,' declared the banker, 'if one has a mind at all.'

'One—no, wait, *immediately*—' the doctor self-corrected, 'if one screws the world as he does.'

'Yes, he does fairly well screw everyone he encounters, now that you phrase it that way. Damnable fellow.' Crespin laughed.

Henry was befuddled for a moment. *Screw?* he echoed in his mind. What was Cedric on about? He knew the banker seemed a passionate fellow, but there was no need in their present conversation for language quite that stron—

Screws.

Views.

He'd said it. Henry had meant to say, 'if one *views* the world as he'—Falstaff—'does.' Apparently, his low opinion of Dick went even deeper than he'd imagined. He felt a bit embarrassed by his *faux pas*—as much for not realising he'd said it as for actually using the word in friendly conversation. But on the other hand, Crespin seemed not to have cared, throwing words like 'damnable' about and steamrolling right into the next round of conversing.

Hm, thought Henry. Maybe he was being too hard on himself. Then again, perhaps he could ill afford not to be.

At any rate, he enjoyed Cedric's company, enjoyed being at this celebration, in its pleasing environment. He'd enjoyed getting to know his host's family better, and looked forward to advising Alex as best he could in medicine, should the boy have need of it. Not only had Falstaff failed to spoil the evening, it had, on the contrary, turned out to be both pleasant and productive, on the whole. He'd made the right decision, coming here.

CHAPTER ELEVEN

Later that same week, some few nights after Cedric Crespin's Christmas party, Dr Richard Falstaff found himself alone inside his bedroom, pondering over what Henry'd said to him. He had drawn the curtains about his bed, covered up with sheets and blankets of finest quality, and sunk into his pillow's soft embrace.

And yet he could not sleep. It had been like this ever since that night—ever since that damnable doctor had revealed that he knew Dick's deepest secret. That this black deed (or deeds), the darkest stain upon his past and person, might yet be made to besmirch his good name—Falstaff would have none of it! But what was he to do? He had to dig up something equally bad about Henry, or he'd stay the one in the disadvantageous position. But what? Falstaff wasn't even sure that such a crime existed. Aside from going to a brothel to find women—an act he himself had committed on many an occasion, and which Henry had, unfortunately, also spotted him doing—he knew of nothing with which he could bring the elder doctor down or even use to even up the stakes. Epilepsy simply paled in comparison.

He hated the threat of exposure and hated being outsmarted even more. Damn it all, how had Henry found out about this?! The only people who'd ever known had been his uncle Harry and himself. Harold had had too much sense to go telling anyone about their escapades, and he, Dick, had never breathed a word of it to—

Wait. He stopped, as he realised who else knew. His mind reeled, his thoughts raced, as he recalled the night that strange and savage beast had beaten the truth out of him, scared him to within less than an inch of his life, there in the bordello, his arms and legs humiliatingly restrained in gaudy yellow bed-curtains. That man, that terrible monster, was the only living being whom Falstaff had ever told. And yet, somehow, Henry'd learned of Dick's dark secret, too. This could mean but one thing.

His heart quickened, his eyes brightened, and he sat bolt upright in bed.

'That's it!' Falstaff exclaimed, pounding his fist once upon the covers in enthusiasm as insight shot him through. *Henry must know the bugger! Why did I not see it before? In order to discern the things he did, why, he'd* have *to know that horrid little man, for he's the only one I told the truth.* The brothel's doors were much too thick, after all, for anyone to have overheard their conversation. And because no one else within his circles had yet so much as hinted at his secret, Dick concluded Henry alone knew—well, Henry and the maniac, of course. And *that* indicated that the devilish man was not simply going about selling the information.

No, Dick reckoned, *there must, then, be some other reason for it, for why would a fiend like that willingly part with such a secret, unless he trusts someone or (more likely) gains something from him in return?*

So what could Henry give this lowly scoundrel of whom Falstaff had run so far afoul? Of course, it could simply have been that Henry knew the blighter or knew a mutual friend that they both trusted. *An illegitimate child of Henry's?* Dick wondered—not of the attacker, for his complexion and features were too different from the doctor's, but of the hypothetical trusted friend. After all, Henry did frequent brothels; he might have a son who knew the knave. But, almost as quickly as it had sprung, Falstaff crushed the thought. For, if the doctor had sired a child out of wedlock, Dick would have known—and much sooner than this, no doubt. Dr Falstaff made it his policy to keep a pulse on any juicy secrets in the ready brothel circles which he frequented (which were smaller than most 'decent' folk might think). Oh, the madams *said* they ensured clients' privacy, but for the right price, one could buy them, just like any other whore. Dick had brought several people down that way, actually, using (fittingly, he thought) the money he'd inherited when Uncle Harry'd died to pay the madams' fees. And yet, not a whisper had Dick ever caught of Henry's darkest deeds, aside from the suspicion that the latter took tarts, too. What, then, could be the connection between the doctor and this devil, the revered and the rogue?

And then it occurred to him, in all its sudden, perverse glory: Henry, the dapper doctor (whom Dick had seen in at least one bordello), never married, handsome (even dandy), with wealth enough to support whomever he pleased...must have taken on the fiery young man as a lover.

'It makes perfect sense,' Falstaff remarked softly. 'It is just as I—' *just as Uncle Harry did with me, so many years ago*, he finished silently. *It seems Henry is his student in more than one avenue*, he reflected.

He thought of his 'uncle', now long dead, gradually superimposed his revised image of Henry onto this picture, then decidedly directed his newly strengthened focus toward one all-consuming goal: *Destroy Henry*. He vowed to find the villain who'd attacked him. Through him, Dick would learn the 'good' doctor's secrets. After that, he'd thoroughly and finally destroy Henry's name, his happiness, his everything.

CHAPTER TWELVE

Henry sat in his dining room, taking his morning tea, blissfully unaware of Falstaff's plotted depredations. It was nigh a month since the Crespins' Christmas party, and the elder doctor had kept up a lively correspondence with the cheerful, high-living entrepreneur turned banker. In the most recent of these letters, Henry had found himself invited to a Mardi Gras or *Carnevale* party, to be held at the home of one Mr Cedric Crespin and family, in celebration of the last 'free' day before the strictures of Lent. It was to be a masquerade, with glorious costumes and spectacular song, a London re-creation of (or attempt at) the more spirited pleasantries of the Continent's south.

Henry was very much looking forward to it. He had cleared his teaching and hospital schedules for the date, and had sent Cedric his R.S.V.P. nearly as soon as he'd received the happy invite. He cherished the thought of dancing and talking and seeing real friends at this grand celebration of gay *Carnevale*. And all without the unpleasant presence of Dick Falstaff, naturally, given Crespin's dislike of the lout. Henry knew he was going to have a marvellous time.

He had given much thought as to what he would wear. He'd settled at last on the costume of the plague doctor, a manner of backhanded admiration for the well-intentioned but woefully ignorant physicians of times past.

He imagined what the party would look like: masked revellers of all sorts swirling about to the tune of Italian songs; Cedric, fat and jolly, at the centre of all the festivities—all against the backdrop of the Crespins' magnificently made-up home. He looked forward to it with eager anticipation.

***

Such was not to be, however—not in Cedric's house, at least. A mere four days before the party, Henry received a short written announcement informing him that there would be a change of venue. The entire affair was now to be held at the home of one Dr Richard Falstaff and not, as had been previously planned, at Mr Crespin's abode.

Henry was shocked as he read the notice over. Not Falstaff again!

How can this be? he wondered impotently, once he was sure his eyes had not deceived him. *It makes no sense!* he thought, aware of Crespin's professed dislike for the man. *Why should the party not be at Cedric's? What on earth has transpired to make this nightmare so?* For he knew he couldn't back out now, could not cancel his plans to attend, without it coming off as an insult to his friend, the banker. Yet he certainly didn't want to even lay eyes on Falstaff...

He heaved a heavy sigh and decided to pay Cedric a visit. Maybe then he could discern what the devil was going on.

***

The reason for the party's relocation became obvious to Henry as soon as he came round Crespin's block. Even from the corner, he could see work crews going back and forth and milling all about the banker's home—or, rather, what was left of it. Shock, coupled with a crushing realisation, assaulted him when he surveyed the scene: Cedric's house was halfway gone to ruin. Apparently, he noticed upon drawing closer, the roof atop the grand dining hall had cracked and given way completely, littering the hardwood floors with masonry debris and not a few large chunks of stone. The remains of rafters lay strewn upon the ground like so much straw—though, judging by the look of things (not to mention all the workers about), the worst of this great fallout had been cleared away by now. He could even see a fellow laying brick, making a wall, or at least rebuilding what remained of one. This was near the top of the cherry staircase, which—miraculously—seemed little the worse for wear. The balcony and roof were both quite gone.

Harry shook his head.

What in God's great name could have caused such strange destruction? And why should it transpire at this time? he wondered to himself. Then he noticed something he had overlooked: the rafter fragments on the floor were singed, as was the panelling still left on the walls. *A fire*, he realised. *That would explain it.* A sudden, awful thought washed over him: What of Cedric? Had he been injured or, worse yet, perished in the blaze? And what of his wife, Mattie, and young Alex?

Henry strode up to one of the workers.

'Excuse me, my good man,' the doctor enquired, 'but can you tell me aught of what's happened here and whether anyone has come to harm?' He looked at the man with a type of polite desperation, as if upon the answer hung the fate of all the world and yet he dared not breach propriety.

The mason looked at him dispassionately, tools still in hand as he replied, rather matter-of-factly, 'Kitchen fire. Spread to the main 'all. Killed a maid and manservant, God rest their souls. The rest got out afore it spread, or wasn't 'ome to begin with. That answer your question, sir?' The man looked like he wanted to fully shift his attention back to the task at hand, but it was clear he also didn't want to show any disrespect to such a gentleman as the one who stood before him.

'Yes, thank you,' he replied, most relieved that the Crespins were safe. It was unfortunate about the manservant and the maid, but such things were not unheard of, and at least his friend hadn't come to harm. *Actually,* he reflected inwardly, *it's rather lucky more were not consumed,* for he could tell the fire must have been fierce, given all the scorch-marks that scarred what remained of the once-grand hall.

'Oh, one last thing, if you would oblige me,' Henry addressed the mason, pulling some money from his pocket as he did so. He had the worker's full attention now.

Nodding, the man turned to face the doctor, leaving his tools lying on the floor. The patch-work he was doing…it could wait.

'Of course, sir,' the workman replied.

'Would you happen to know,' Henry asked him, 'where Mr Cedric Crespin and his family reside at present?'

***

During his conversation with Cedric at one of London's better hotels (to which the informative mason had only too happily directed him), it became clear to Henry what exactly had happened. As the banker corroborated, a fire had indeed broken out in the Crespins' kitchen, spreading swiftly to the main, grand hall, where it had awakened the family dog. The loyal hound had raised the alarm, making a beeline for Alex's bedroom and waking the boy before he'd even smelled smoke. A couple of servants, roused by the animal's cries, had thereupon seen plumes of jet black drifting through the halls. One of the pair had gone to wake Mr and Mrs Crespin, while the other had alerted the remaining household staff to the growing blaze. Unfortunately, not all had been awakened—*warned*—in time. The two closest to the kitchen had burned alive.

'Dreadful, that,' Cedric commented, his voice wavering slightly.

'And there, but for the grace of God, go we,' Mattie added. Utter seriousness pervaded her entire visage. 'When I think what might have happened...' She trailed off, then looked concernedly at Alex, then to the dog, and back again. Her eyes conveyed all the warmth and worry of a mother who had almost lost her child.

'No use dwelling on things that didn't, though, dearest,' Cedric reassured. 'Besides, crews are rebuilding as we speak. The house'll be ship-shape soon enough, good as new—no, *better* than that!—you'll see. Though not, I'm afraid, in time for *Carnevale*,' he concluded with a wistful air.

'I see,' said Henry. 'That explains the change in venue. Yet I was wondering, and I hope you'll not think ill of me for asking this, but...was there, by any chance, a location available which was a little more... How shall I put this...?'

'Not Falstaff's?' Crespin finished for him.

'Well...yes,' Henry admitted sheepishly, and gave his friend a nod.

'Bugger had me in a bind,' Crespin recounted, drawing from Mattie a request of 'Cedric, *please!*' as she covered their son's ears. Reluctantly softening his language, the banker continued. It turned out that, a day or so after the fire, he had been speaking with a friend of his at a social club about what had transpired. This chum had thereupon expressed his sympathies, as well as his regret (as he supposed the Crespins' plans for festive *Carnevale* would, by necessity, have to be discarded). It had been at this point that both were suddenly made aware of Dr Falstaff's presence in the club, as he had then joined their conversation quite loudly (so that all gathered there could hear). He had saccharinely expressed his sympathies. Next, with a smile on his lips and a look of cunning in his eye as he anticipated the banker's displeasure, Dick had proudly offered up his own abode, that there the grandiose masquerade might take place after all—though only with Mr Crespin's approval, of course. Cedric had been left no recourse but to graciously accept, for several of his invitees sat there within the room, and all had heard the doctor's generous proposal. It would have been the height of rudeness to refuse, especially in so public a gentlemanly venue.

Thus it came to pass that the formerly light-hearted Cedric's celebration was to be held in the home of the eminent, ever-infuriating Dr Falstaff—still paid for, of course, by Mr

Crespin, and still attended by his invitees. *All* the invitees. And that included Henry.

It occurred to Harry, on his way home, that his plague doctor costume was going to be very fitting indeed. He'd have to do his best while at the gathering not to be 'infected' by Falstaff's effects upon him personally. Otherwise, he might unintentionally let slip his anger at the man in public. One simply did *not* insult one's host, however displeasurable he might be. God, how he detested that man... This was supposed to have been a pleasant party, a dandy masquerade. How had he got himself into this mess? And his mind said to him then, *Physician, heal thyself.*

***

Dick, meanwhile, had been rather busy. After his all-too-public conversation with Crespin, Falstaff had had all sorts of tasks to occupy his time. There were special chefs to line up, many rooms yet to be decorated, and several other things besides (which he was glad he was not paying for). Yes, he'd gone all out with this endeavour—*his* party now, not Cedric's, even though the latter was still footing the bill—and he wanted it to go off without a hitch. He did intend to antagonise Crespin a bit in private—any fool who'd be friends with a devoted student of his uncle's, like Henry, deserved it—but it was the doctor he was truly after. Dick had noticed, upon their last encounter, that, despite the revelation that this fellow knew Falstaff's deepest and most shameful secret, it had been *Dick* who had made *Henry* unseasonably uncomfortable—so much so that the elder chap had grown quietly angry, acting not unlike an unmannerly woman—not the reverse. Falstaff realised that he apparently had a singular ability to get under the doctor's skin—even more so than with most of the other victims he'd targeted for his abuses in times past.

This, Dick reflected, *gives me just the edge I need to triumph yet*, even though, despite his best efforts, he had been able to find neither hide nor hair of the small, roguish man from the bordello. Thus, Falstaff got it into his head that, as the *de facto* host of the party, he would at some point take Henry aside to speak to him in private. The elder doctor, seeing as it would be Falstaff's home they were in, would have no choice but to comply. Thereafter, once out of earshot of the other guests, Dick aimed to do his savage best at rousing Henry's ire. Then, at the key moment, when Denman's old student was no longer in rational control of himself, Falstaff would turn the conversation round, back to secrets, shadows, and shame, and—more than likely—the senior doctor, in that frame of mind, was bound to let *something* slip.

And then, Dick thought with anticipatory relish, *then, I shall have him.* He smiled—a most unfriendly, *predatory* smile.

CHAPTER THIRTEEN

The day of the party arrived, and Henry hit upon a grand idea: he couldn't avoid the affair outright, but he could certainly cut his visit short. He had it in his head to feign sickness not long after his planned arrival. Being a doctor, it would be fairly easy to fake the appropriate symptoms. He would have liked to skip the soiree entirely, seeing as Falstaff was in charge of it, but he wouldn't have felt right just leaving Cedric in the lurch to deal with Dick himself for the whole evening. Besides, another invitee had seen Henry just that morning, so the decision was moot. He'd simply take his leave as early as he could, once everyone had had a chance to notice his attendance. He hoped he'd be able to do so without Dr Falstaff's ill attentions—or, at the very least, without affording the dubious Dick the opportunity to provoke another episode in him.

And so it was that Henry, mask in hand, with fever-sounding cough now primed and ready, set out this chill, clear night for Dr Falstaff's.

***

He was a bit taken aback when he first laid eyes upon the younger doctor's posh abode. This house, while not too exceedingly large in and of itself, was located in a part of London where a lodging of its size was usually unheard of. It was, in fact, a rather grand townhouse, dwarfing its nearby neighbours by embarrassing margins.

The ostentatious nature of the scale of this great dwelling was nothing compared to what lay inside. Having disembarked from his cab, Henry, upon entering, beheld what might have been described as 'over the top'…but merely as a matter of understatement. From the heavy, ornate carvings to the shimmering chandeliers, from the almost comically massive candelabras to the umbrella stand made of an elephant's foot, the place bespoke the magnificence, the gaudiness, the pomp and self-importance, the very soul and spirit of the modern, Victorian age. It sickened Harry even as it awed and overwhelmed him.

Babylon, I have seen thee, he reflected silently.

In addition to the house's usual overabundance of decoration, a few new flourishes had been recently added: masks—row upon row upon row of them—lined every wall, nook, doorframe, hearth, and every last low window (in the public areas, at least). Masks had been hung along the rails of the stairway leading to the upper floors. Masks were everywhere, of every colour, shape, and size, some made in only Venice, some from French *Indochine* or faraway Taipei, and some—the most unusual of all—of unforeseen, unwished-for, bizarre and local make. Henry concluded that Falstaff had simply wished to fill up *all* the spaces, judging by the odd look and inferior quality of the ones Dick must've commissioned locally. Quantity, not quality, had been the prime objective, Henry thought.

How brash! he muttered inwardly. He felt downright sophisticated in his sombre plague doctor ensemble.

Henry's presence was announced as he entered the largest room, which was of only moderate size (as this *was* a townhouse), and was therefore extremely crowded. It struck him as counterintuitive to broadcast someone's name at a masquerade ball, but then, Falstaff never was that respectful of anyone he couldn't use, and Harry supposed that went for the Venetians and their time-honoured traditions as well.

Falstaff, meanwhile, had heard his servant blare out the (plague) doctor's arrival, and began to disentangle himself from the conversation in which he was currently engaged.

Henry, happily enough, soon found a familiar face in the form of one Cedric Crespin, whose costume chanced to leave his countenance uncovered. He was dressed as 'the Doctor' of the *commedia dell'arte*, a stock character famous for his braggadocio, pedantic antics, and high opinion of himself.

'In honour of our host,' he whispered to Harry, once the latter had revealed himself to Cedric. 'If I can't host the party, then I'll still bloody well enjoy it, at the least.'

Henry concurred.

'Would that I had thought of such a witty costume choice myself, my friend,' he told the Doctor. 'Though you're rather brave to actually go through with it.'

'Brave? I? No, just foolish,' Crespin countered, 'though not so foolish as to let them *all* know,' he informed Harry, gesturing discreetly at the rest of the assembled. 'Only a select few,' he declared, putting his finger to his lips in a sign for silent secrecy. Lowering his voice still further, he added, 'I think our host can pick up what I mean, though. Yet it's a small revenge, quite small, for having to endure him.'

Henry, who had taken off his mask to talk to Cedric, found himself of like mind, and said as much. 'The fellow is insufferable,' he told him. 'I plan to leave as early as I may—if you don't mind being left here on your own with him.'

'No, no, completely understandable, old chap,' Crespin reassured. 'Besides, I'll only stay to goad him.'

Harry smiled.

The smile vanished as he noticed a face creep up behind his mischievous cohort. He felt the sudden urge to put his mask back on, but then thought others might mark the move as rude, so he simply stood there, feeling overly exposed as Falstaff quickly closed the shrinking space between them.

The younger doctor was dressed in the costume of Brighella, the clever, devious servant in the *commedia*'s cast.

'Henry,' he began, in a falsely gracious tone, 'so good to see you here, and looking so *well*, too. I trust you are enjoying my masked ball?' He glanced at Cedric, who looked as if he were just about to say something about this, then speedily went on, 'Oh, Cedric old boy, so terribly sorry; this is *your* party, of course, even if I *am* the one hosting it. You paid for it, after all…every last farthing, I believe.'

'God looks out for fools,' Crespin returned. 'It's small wonder you're so bloody lucky, I do say!'

'*I* am simply smart enough to take advantage of a happy situation when it comes my way.'

'And ruin it,' put in Cedric.

'Look around, dear Mr Crespin. Look at all the guests, the splendid decorations, the many masks upon the walls. Does it look "ruined" to you? I think not.'

'*I think not,*' repeated Henry in his mind. *Amen to that, you blighter. You* don't *think. Not about anyone but yourself, at any rate.* But he didn't have the chance to slip these words into the conversation (and likely wouldn't have done so anyway) before Falstaff continued:

'It seems to me they're all having a grand old time. I must say, this little soiree has done much to improve my standing in these circles. I really should thank you, Cedric.' He gave a nasty smile.

The banker, struggling not to speak his mind, had turned red, even through his face-paint.

'You are a damnable cur and you will die miserable and alone!' Crespin blurted.

Thankfully, the party's musicians drowned him out with strings and drums. Falstaff heard him, though, as did Harry. Whereas the latter grew distressed upon seeing Cedric so upset, the former merely congratulated himself on a job well done. If he could rattle Crespin, Henry would be a breeze.

The banker left Dick's presence in a huff, declaring, 'You are worth neither my time nor my breath. I've played this damn charade quite long enough.' And with that, he was gone, entirely forgetting the fact that, in his clouded, angry, fed-up state of mind, he'd just abandoned Henry to the lion in its den.

'Well,' Falstaff remarked, 'how amusing. It seems the rotund "Doctor" has no manners.'

'Nor do you,' said Henry, finally, appalled at what the 'Brighella' had just done. To Harry's mind, there was no call for that sort of behaviour, absolutely no call! And toward someone as right and honourable as Cedric—a decent chap, who was paying for this whole affair, to boot!

'Oh?' queried Dick. 'As if you were so very different. Why, I've witnessed angry women behave better than you did when last we conversed. I'm afraid you have no room to speak upon these matters, my dear doctor.' He glanced at Henry's costume. 'You know, that outfit really is rather appropriate on you, given your obvious inferiority in the medical sciences.'

'I beg your pardon!' declared Henry. 'I studied under Denman, just as you did.' Here his thoughts went inwardly, *Well, not just as you did, you harpyish homosexual*, but outwardly he added only, 'And I'll have you know I perform chemistry as well, and could also practice law, if I so chose. I am perfectly qualified in many fields, and what's more, I am financially secure enough to pursue whatsoever interest I please, quite apart from any monies such jobs would pay. Whatever I do, I do because I *choose*.'

'Oh, how terribly impressive,' Falstaff said sarcastically. 'You can fight in petty civil suits or mix up draughts of laudanum. However shall I stand before your grandeur?'

'I have "mixed up" far more than any paltry palliative, far more than your dense, petty mind can know—could ever *hope* to know!' countered Harry.

The elder doctor did not notice, but a crowd began to form at this last comment, drawn by the volume of Henry's declaration and the obvious exchange of venom taking place between the two. Even the band had stopped playing in order to listen to their quarrel.

'At least I do not waste my time, nor take up precious space on Earth, defending a worthless mentor and following his example to the last.' Dick knew this jab at Denman would prick Harry, and hoped he'd crack and thus let something slip—especially regarding Henry's apparent predilection for younger men, a fact Falstaff implied by his last statement. After all, Falstaff's 'uncle' had had the same, and Dick now hoped Harry would make mention of the rogue from the bordello, thus exposing his shame to all who watched, and in this way letting his good name come to ruin—*by his own words.*

'You know *nothing,*' Harry snarled through gritted teeth, his face growing a deep reddish-pink. 'Whatever he may've done, Denman was still a *decent fellow*—it is his example I follow when I tend the poor, the sick, the injured—and that is something more than you will ever be!' Henry's brow darkened as the dam began to break. 'You are nothing but a spineless, bullying, self-important cur who poisons everything he's ever touched!' he spat. 'You call yourself a doctor?! You trample down compassion for your bloody self-amusement! All people are to you but things, just *things* to make you feel the least bit better about your accursed self by fooling them or knocking them down, but you cannot truly *feel* at all! You are a liar, a cad, a bloody, God-damned hypocrite! If anyone sees through you, down he goes! And for what? *What?* Damn it, man, don't speak to me of wasting the world's space. If there's *anyone* on God's green Earth who ought just disappear, then it is *you*, Dick Falstaff; it's *not I*—ohhh...' Harry trailed off as he finished his tirade, suddenly not looking very well. He blanched and held his temples. Slowly, a tremor began to creep its way from the core of his being to the outer layers of his flesh. At the same time, a wave of nausea welled up inside his body like the tide.

Run, was the only thought he could manage, for he knew he had to get out of this place, away from all these people...away from Falstaff.

He took off with an unsteady gait down a hallway just off the main room, dropping his mask on the dance floor in his haste.

CHAPTER FOURTEEN

Falstaff watched with concealed amusement and glee as the doctor raged, making a hysterical fool of himself. Outwardly, Dick put on an appearance of shock and indignation. Only a very careful observer would have noticed Falstaff's eyes narrow in anticipation as he saw the first signs of oncoming epilepsy lay hold of Henry. When Harry took off running, his host followed just behind, relishing this moment and joyfully anticipating the fruits of his labours. He'd have conclusive proof of Henry's ailment, and likely several witnesses to boot. Indeed, he could even now hear behind him the hurried footfalls of some concerned or curious guests. Dick marched to the doorway through which Henry had just fled.

This led to Falstaff's drawing room, complete with fireplace, table, sofas, chairs... but what attracted Dick's present fickle attention as he strode into this otherwise normal room was its clear-as-crystal window, which overlooked a mid-sized garden plot enclosed by a courtyard just behind the house.

The window was open.

'Damn!' Falstaff cursed aloud, then realised Henry couldn't have gone far.

He dispatched one of his housemaids to check back round the courtyard, while Dick illumed the guests who had caught up:

'It seems the good doctor has stepped out for some fresh air,' he said sardonically, with a gesture at the draft-allowing casement. He was sure the servant would find Henry helplessly twitching in the midst of a seizure any moment now. He was a mite disappointed that he hadn't found out any additional name-staining secrets from the erstwhile plague doctor—and after all that pleasant, hard work, too!—but it would be enough to have some of the upper crust witness Henry in the throes of his current bout of personal weakness...not to mention the histrionic display the man had given back inside the main hall. With any luck, no one would ever *want* to talk to Henry after this, and it wouldn't matter even if he tried to tell Dick's secret.

'Excuse me, sir,' the servant he had sent caught his attention as she returned from the rear part of the house.

'Yes?' asked Falstaff, eagerly. 'Where is he?'

She looked downward, then said something very softly and apologetically in a low tone.

'Speak up, woman; we can't hear you!' her master commanded, indicating the guests who stood nearby him.

'I'msorrysirIcouldn'tfindhimthere,there's no-onetheresir!' she exclaimed, all rapid-fire, then turned her head away (as if from an anticipated blow).

'What?' was all Dick managed, baffled. 'Not there?' His eyes turned curious then, in turn, enraged. 'What do you bloody well mean there's nobody there, you lousy wen—?' He stopped himself, remembering the others in the room.

'Does anyone know where our plague doctor's gone?' he asked them, pleasantly enough, changing the subject as quickly as his tone. But no one did, nor could any find him, not even as the party came to a close and all the guests and hired hands went home. The doctor, it seemed, had vanished into the very aether. He could nowhere be found—though a couple of searchers did report another open window, while Dick himself saw one of his masks missing.

***

Falstaff puzzled over all of this as he prepared for bed later that night. The situation quite perplexed him.

'It makes no sense,' he stated, standing before his upper-storey window as he put his nightcap on. 'I had him—I had him right there,' he muttered to himself. 'They were going to see his malady! His name was to be ruined!'

'The only thing that shall be ruined is *you*!' howled a voice from close behind him.

As Dick began to turn around, he felt the staggering impact of something hard and cold as it hit the right side of his head. Porcelain bits scattered on the ground, the sad remains of what had once been a favourite china vase.

'What the bloody—?' Dick began, hunched over with his hands clutching his head.

'Bloody indeed,' came that same, too-familiar voice, as a pain pulsed through Falstaff's side. It felt like he'd been struck with something blunt—again. The vision in his right eye went red, and he realised his forehead must be bleeding. With his good eye, he turned to face his assailant.

There he was. The man was small of stature, dressed in clothes of black, the accoutrements and gloves too large for him, though they somehow stayed upon him all the same. A broken clock which had once adorned Falstaff's mantel (and which had just been used to smite Dick's ribs) lay in ruin close beside the strange man. His skin seemed at once swarthy and yet pale, as if unhealthy. But what caught Doctor Falstaff's prime attention was what the stranger wore upon his face: a mask—a most unusual, unnerving mask—a mask of unknown local English make that, by the look of it, should never have been crafted. It concealed this villain's nose, cheeks, temples, forehead, this mask of deepest black with flecks of crimson round its edges. Red lined the eyes as well. And, just through these twin holes, where the windows of the soul were to be seen, lay two cruel pools of dark, stark, rage-filled hate.

Dick recognised him immediately as the man from the bordello. Even as the doctor felt his ribcage start to bruise, his mind howled out to kill this man or flee him. He had no clue what the blighter was doing here, but he was not about to be his victim once again!

And so, as the devilish man rushed toward him, Falstaff lurched around to take him on. Even in his current, battered state, Dick thought he could best him; the rogue was wiry, but still small and slight of build—as if, when young, he had been undernourished. It should have been quite easy...but it wasn't.

'Die, you hypocritical dog!' the madman hissed, and sprang.

Unfortunately for him, however, his leap ended not in a tackling down of Falstaff but rather with an impact square across the latter's fist. No sooner had the maniac fallen to the floor than he kicked Dick harshly in the shin. Halfway hopping about, the doctor made a frantic grab at his attacker but succeeded only in ripping off his mask. This revealed the villain's face, a sight that unnerved Falstaff even as he saw that the rogue's nose was bleeding. That punch *had* done some good.

Apparently, it hadn't done enough.

'Look upon it, mongrel!' the fiend raged, indicating his unpleasant visage. 'It shall be the last thing that you see!' Having risen from the ground, he began to kick savagely at the hobbling doctor until Falstaff lay mewling on the floor. Yet still he did not stop this brutal onslaught until, much sooner than expected, he heard cries from the stairwell: shouts of alarm from Dick's household servants, who'd heard the noise the two had made in their scuffle.

'Damn!' cursed the assailant, glancing toward the hallway. He knew the stairs were not that far removed. Thinking quickly, he threw open Falstaff's window, then gave his victim a most frightening grin.

The doctor, though thoroughly bruised up, was still quite conscious—a fact he rather regretted. He'd much preferred never to have seen that dark and piercing stare, that hate-filled smile, the blood dyeing the blackguard's teeth deep red. And Dick *certainly* wished that he'd been unaware when the foul sadist did what he did next.

With a heave of strength that could only have been born of desperation, the horrid man hoisted Falstaff to his feet (though not without some effort) and then—then!—shoved him out the window frame, towards the garden below. But Dick's tormentor kept hold of him as he did so, and they both thus hurtled through the air. Falstaff was confused for the slow-moving split second that it took them to fall in tandem, but the intruder's purpose soon became too cruelly clear. The last thing Dick remembered was a sudden, jarring impact as he stared up at the villain's vengeful frame. Falstaff felt like he'd been hit by a large, brick wall. (More accurately, he had hit a solid brick floor: the near part of the courtyard, hard as stone.) The last vision to greet him ere his thoughts all slipped away was the stark, fearsome image of the madman's fiendish face, his unrelenting, rage-filled eyes impaling Dick's black soul.

Then all the doctor saw went black as well.

CHAPTER FIFTEEN

A pair of Falstaff's servants were the first upon the scene of his fall. One even caught a glimpse from behind of their employer's nemesis as he fled, and gave chase to him into the dark street, but soon lost sight of the light-footed fiend in inky-black alleyways. And so the tracker came back at a loss. He found the other staff trying to tend their injured master. One had sent for a doctor, to see if their employer would survive this terrible ordeal. Another went to fetch London's police, appalled that anyone (even so harsh a master) should be so cruelly assailed.

When the requested doctor first arrived, he took a moment to take in what had happened. After the examination of his unconscious patient, he determined that the latter's injuries, while painful, were not lethal (though there were some bones that needed to be set). Dick was still knocked out cold when the sawbones left after instructing Falstaff's servants to inform him when their master should awake. Some of the stronger men in Falstaff's service carried their bruised and bandaged master into a guest bedroom, shutting the door to Dick's usual sleeping quarters, lest the intruder dare return. Falstaff himself they guarded through the night.

***

The misanthropic miscreant who'd nearly done Dick in meanwhile ran round the frigid streets of London, trying hard to stay away from view. He made his way through quiet squares and lonely churchyards, through death-still thoroughfares and pitch-black alleyways stained with grime. He stuck close to the shadows at all times.

His mind raced. Where would he go? If any were to find him, he'd be killed! And come daylight, he would have no place to hide. The shadows were barely doing the job as it was; the stars and moon and gas lights were, tonight, unobscured by any fog. He prayed no night patrolman would pass by.

As if to spite him, a peeler appeared, crossing the corner at the end of the lane. It was only by the slimmest of margins that the malicious madman managed to duck into a shallow alleyway in time enough to miss the lawman's gaze. The fugitive breathed a sigh of relief as the policeman opted to turn left and walk in the opposite direction of the criminal's hiding place. Taking his chances while the bobby's back was turned, the scoundrel fled, with odd, light, purposefully muted steps, dashing down a cross-street lest the copper chance to turn around. This, as it turned out, was quite fortuitous, for the night patrolman did just that, not moments afterward. Of course, by such time, the ruffian was long gone.

***

It was nearly half-past midnight when the shadowy, violent villain finally came upon his chosen destination. This location had occurred to him as a possible safe-house not long after his near run-in with the law. The almost-encounter had set his mind to thinking on that subject—the law—and he'd realised in short order where he ought to try to go. He had even formulated a plan of sorts while on his way. It wasn't foolproof—there was no guarantee he'd be admitted entry, a servant might raise the alarm, the party to whom he desired to speak might turn him away forever or call Scotland Yard himself—but, given the limited options available to him in these tenuous circumstances, this plan seemed his best bet.

Upon arriving at his destination, the man who had so savagely fought Falstaff earlier that evening paused a moment before the door, readying himself. Then he knocked thrice, rapidly. Immediately thereafter, he took his place behind a column of the porch, for he was slight enough not to be noticed, in this manner, by anyone who should come to the door. He waited a few minutes.

Nothing happened.

Frustrated, he repeated the process over, knocking much more loudly than before. Within all of a minute, the building's door unbolted. He tensed, hearing the sliding of the lock. A half-moment later, the cloth-covered head of a servant emerged, peering cautiously out from under its nightcap at the starlight-swathed street.

The servant remembered nothing next except seeing stars. These, however, were no heavenly bodies. Rather, they resulted from a resounding blow struck by one who belonged far from any heaven. The poor servant knew nothing but black.

The desperate devil stepped quickly and quietly over the manservant's motionless body and into the home's front entrance hall. So far, so good. He was in.

***

At nearly the same moment that the downstairs servant had met with the impact which rendered him immobile, someone in an upstairs bedroom of the house had startled out of sleep. He knew not why. Yet awake he was now, wide awake, as if he'd just evaded some strange nightmare by becoming conscious of the room around him, real as always.

Yet still he felt a twinge of unease, a knowledge in his gut that things were somehow *off*. He certainly wouldn't be able to get back to sleep.

Resigning himself to his fate, he decided to head toward his business room to get a head start on his work. As he descended the stairs, however, he thought he heard a door click into place, followed by a flash of odd, light footsteps. He looked about, eyes straining to make out anything strange within the darkened house. And there he spied it: near the doorway, in the foyer, lay a still and crumpled form. He couldn't really discern any details, not from here. He made his way down the few remaining steps, then traversed the foyer. He realised almost immediately that it was Carson, the one of his household staff who'd always been the latest man to bed.

He didn't have time to think much further on this, for, unnoticed, a black-clad form had crept up right behind him, crossing from beneath the balconette. The would-be examiner found a hand over his mouth before he could so much as utter a syllable, while another hand restrained him from behind.

'John,' a hoarse and gravelly voice whispered in his ear, 'I need to talk to you.'

Shivers ran up the poor lawyer's spine. That voice—he'd thought he'd never hear its sound again. He'd thought the fiend who owned it utterly destroyed—by Henry's hand, no less! For John had seen this blighter on the ground, had seen him twitching from the pains of death, had been there when the body had been carted away! And yet, now here he was, (sur)real as anything, violating John's own darkened home, spiriting the lawyer swiftly away from the foyer, down a hallway, through a door, and into his drawing room, at which point the door clicked shut behind them and John felt himself released.

'Have a seat,' he was instructed.

The lawyer glanced quickly toward the windows.

'John,' the voice commanded him again, this time with the touch of a growl to it, 'Have. A. *Seat.*' His would-be captor gestured toward a chair and the sofa. Having seemingly intercepted what it was John had been thinking, he also moved himself purposefully between the attorney and the clear-paned avenues of escape.

John sat, keeping a wary eye on the fellow before him. The initial shock of seeing him here—alive—was beginning to fade, and this gave the lawyer's senses the chance to notice something strange (well, strang*er*) about the bloke: he appeared a few inches taller since last John had seen him. This didn't, of course, render him the least bit tall, or of even average height, but it was still an odd and, to the attorney's mind, disturbing new development…in part because of what else it might signify.

Regardless, he did not relish being at this man's mercy. The blighter was a wanted murderer—or at least he had been, until his 'death'. But it seemed now even *that* had been an act.

A most convincing act, thought John, *and perhaps unintentional. I suppose it is possible that Henry, in his haste, might have miscalculated how much poison to stuff down this devil's throat. And the police, as I recall, stated that the body must have been given over to some anatomy class or other. So it is entirely possible, however improbable, that he* did *survive his 'death' without the highest lawman any the wiser.* John determined he'd soon remedy that.

And with that, he made a beeline for the door, calculating that he'd reach it before his captor, who, seeing John seated and apparently complacent, had begun to pace restlessly near the windows, on the opposite side of the room.

This calculation was off. John, though not arthritic—he was actually quite spry, for a man of his years—could not compete with the unexpected speed with which the madman dashed his way across the room, throwing himself between John and the door.

'Damn it, man!' he cursed the just-foiled lawyer. 'Sit down and *listen*!' With this, he shoved John onto the nearby couch.

It seemed to the attorney there was no choice—at least, for now.

Very well, then, he concluded to himself. *I shall hear this blackguard out, and thereby, perhaps, gain his trust. Then I may be able to simply walk out of this room when he departs—if he departs—and inform Scotland Yard that he yet lives.*

'Very well,' John told his captor. 'What is it you're so eager to discuss?'

***

It soon became clear to John that the fellow was positively out of his mind, though with enough wits yet about him to prove dangerous, and intimately familiar with John's friend, Henry, and the doctor's unfortunate, occasional fits of drug-induced fancy. Why, even now, his captor rambled on with impatient preciseness and in such detail as only a close confidant should know. It was obvious to John this lunatic had forced poor Harry to tell him his life story when he'd held the doctor hostage some eleven or so months past. How the villain had evaded capture for this long, God only knew, but John intended to set that error straight. Now he had only to talk the murderous reprobate out of his vicinity.

'I see,' the shrewd attorney said, agreeing with his captor. 'Then I shall do exactly as you say. I owe a friend no less.'

At this, the madman's entire demeanour altered. No longer was he angry with frustration, no more did indignation mar his pale and moody brow. Instead, a yelp of pure elation rose up from his throat; it turned into a cackle midway out. Playfully, he pushed John off the couch, tossing the throw-pillow that'd been behind the lawyer into the air. He caught it, one-handed, on its return way down, then plopped it back into its rightful place.

'I suppose you will not mind if I stay here, hidden, today?' he asked his host, with a sneering sort of self-entitlement that tainted even his joy.

'Naturally,' returned John, relieved the maniac had taken the bait. Now all that remained was to wait until this criminal was hidden away, then contact the authorities and let them reel him in. 'I believe you'll find the attic undisturbed. There is one window, though I don't advise going near it if you want to keep clear of any prying eyes.'

'Of course. Naturally. And you'll do everything else besides, just as I've said?'

'Precisely as you've said.'

'Grand! Then I'll go up straight away.' He crossed over to the door, intending to go through it and up the staircase and, from there, to the attic above. Yet he hesitated, turned around, and cast a look at John.

As the man regarded him, John felt, he knew not why, that he had been found out. The dark eyes of the fugitive seemed to plumb down into his soul. Yet, he needn't have worried.

'At least,' the strange guest pronounced solemnly, with a trace of bitterness, '*you*, John, I can count upon.' And with that, he took his leave.

John waited till he heard the fellow's footfall vanish up the steps, then waited some time more, just to be safe.

CHAPTER SIXTEEN

By the time a recovered Mr Carson returned with the police (as per his master's instructions), John noticed it was nearly ten past three. A fog had crept in, rolling through damp byways and obliterating every star in the sky.

Upstairs, John's uninvited guest slept fitfully, entangling himself in his robes of black, his sweating palms soaking his dark gloves through.

He awoke with a start, barely stifling a scream, sitting bolt upright as he gasped for breath. Perspiration trickled from his forehead, the salty drops creeping down his pale face until, at last, they came into his mouth. This unanticipated taste, coupled with the sight of the attic around him, reminded him where he was and how he'd come there.

But, Lord, what a nightmare he'd had! He'd dreamed he had awoken, the day bright, to birds' soft chirrupings outside his room. He'd come down and had breakfast with his current, pleasant host, a feast of tea and crumpets, ham and eggs, jam, butter, toast, with sandwiches and scones thrown in just for good measure.

'For me?' he'd asked John, to which the latter had nodded.

'You are my honoured guest,' the lawyer had told him with a smile while servants had pulled out two chairs for them.

'Lovely,' he'd answered, the indescribably sweet feeling of being honoured, wanted, and appreciated—*as he was*—making his dark face bright. 'Bloody lovely.' He'd sat down to eat then, starting on his breakfast as if famished, cutting the meat and slathering his toast with purple jam. As he'd dug into a scone, though, something had seemed not quite right. His vision had blurred; he'd been unable to get the damned baked good into focus, able to make out only a pale, doughy mass. A doughy, *squirming* mass. His vision had cleared just as he'd prepared to take a bite.

Maggots! Squirming, disgusting *maggots* in his scone! He'd cried out in shock and horror, only to see John smugly looking on. The attorney hadn't touched *his* breakfast. John had seemed to recede into the distance, knowing something he would not let on. Just then, four strong policemen had burst right through the front door. (Somehow, the dining table had miraculously moved itself from its usual resting area to the foyer.) The inky-blue-clad bobbies had laid hold of him, dragging him away, away, toward the gallows.

'John!' he'd cried out. 'John!' But the man had refused to even look at him.

And suddenly, with that, he had arrived. The hangman's beam had shot high, high into the sky, its silhouette stark black against the sun as it'd loomed over him.

The hangman had put a noose around his neck as the four large lawmen had held him back despite his struggling. They'd let him dangle then. And just as the fateful knot had begun to tighten round his throat, his hands uselessly pulling at the ropes that'd bound them behind his back—just then, at the precise moment that he'd felt his life begin to ebb away in this unpleasant, midair drowning, beyond the reach of any who might've helped him, he'd seen the executioner pull back his ebon hood. What had lain beneath had taken his last breath away.

'Tis John. The revelation had pierced him through.

He'd awakened then, nearly screaming, sweat beading on his brow and down his face. And then, just after he'd remembered where he was, had realised it had only been a dream, *then* he saw something that made his hackles rise and his stomach sink. Out the attic window, just barely, through the fog, he thought he caught a glimpse of that most unique of helmets, the kind worn only by London's finest. Not half a second later, he heard a door unlock—the front door, he imagined, as the attic window faced the street. There followed furtive voices, several hushed and hurried tones. Then he heard it, the most dread-inducing, fearsome word of all: 'Gallows.' And the voice that had said it… was John's.

Assumptions

It seemed his own dark nightmare had come true. His last hope had become his executioner, his deathblow and his Judas all in one.

He heard the lawmen sneaking up the steps. They'd soon be here! What could he do?!

Apparently, the police soon discovered, he could flee out the window. Hearing a loud crash, they rushed up the remaining flight of stairs, only to find the attic's lonely opening devoid of most of its glass.

Several of the lot cursed at their luck.

'He must've fled to the street!' said one of them, looking through the window's sad remains.

'From this height?' questioned another. 'He must've broke his leg, then, else he ain't human.'

'No!' returned the first, rushing away from the window and right past his comrades. 'The porch's roof is right below that window. He must've jumped there and then to the ground. Now come on, lads!' he exclaimed with urgent vexation, descending the stairs as quickly as he could. 'If we hurry, we might lay hold of him yet!'

With that, the bobbies chased their way into the night, searching almost till the dawn had come. They came up empty-handed.

But while the lawmen were thus occupied, a strange sight could be seen in John's drafty attic. A large, brown-leather trunk, half-filled with musty books, appeared to move of its own accord. The hinged top started up a couple of times, then finally swung free, disturbing dust as its impact jarred the creaky wooden floorboards. With a sneeze, its scrawny occupant emerged.

God, that was a close one, he thought as he rose up from the box and stepped to the floor. Dust and paper particles flew clear as he shook himself clean. *What a stroke of luck to find this stupid trunk*, he observed to himself. *And at least John's bloody large copy of* Paradise Lost *proved good for* something.

He'd taken it out to make room for himself in the trunk, then (in his opinion) put it to much better use. He imagined it still lay somewhere in the street below, along with several random bits of glass.

'Bloody stupid policemen. Thank God,' he muttered quietly, then started down the stairway, wondering if John or anyone would notice him on his way out. As luck had it, both the lawyer and Mr Carson had gone with the police (for questioning as well as to aid in the search), and so there were naught but a few groggy servants in the house as he departed, blending his way once more into the foggy streets of London.

The vapours had grown thicker by this time, a natural phenomenon he turned to his advantage. This grey pea soup wouldn't trouble him in the least; he knew his way from John's home, knew precisely how to get where he was headed, even though he hadn't paid the establishment a visit in some months. It was the only place he could think of that might admit him at this hour. He imagined he might encounter a spot of trouble, thanks to his reputation there. *But,* he reasoned, *it is nothing a little money cannot fix. I shall simply have to retain a sense of... civility. A necessary evil, I suppose, given my damnable circumstances.* He hoped he wouldn't have to kowtow too badly, else he might lose all control of his ire.

CHAPTER SEVENTEEN

He arrived at his destination while it was still dark out, though the interior of the place was warmly lighted enough. The décor here was of bright colour, too: Red pillows on crimson couches met the eye before burgundy drapes with gold-hued fringe. At the bar, a few patrons were carousing, each with his chosen woman by his side. All three couples soon left this room, however, departing for other, more private quarters, leaving the madam and Heather alone at the counter. It was just after this had occurred that the freshly escaped fugitive happened into the place. In the blink of an eye, he knocked out the newly hired porter with a surprise uppercut and made his way swiftly toward the two.

'God's balls!' cursed the madam in shock, a flood of anger and panic rising up from within and showing itself plainly on her face.

Heather simply blanched, petrified.

'Now, now,' the newcomer chided, his voice full of unintentional menace. 'There's no need for such...*theatricality.*' He strode up to the bar, the madam backing away instinctively as he did so. Heather was so afraid she couldn't move. (This, as it happened, put the poor girl not three feet to the right of the new arrival.)

Assumptions

The madam looked at him fearfully, leaning back against the far inside edge of the semicircular counter, in a not-so-unconscious effort to get as far away from him as possible. After all, there was no telling *what* he might do...

To her surprise, he plunked a sizeable sum of cash upon her counter. She regarded him quizzically, the wariness still visible in her eyes.

'What's that about?' she asked suddenly, and with a bit too much force, as if she had been holding her breath in fear and then let it out too quickly, in one gust.

'A gesture of...' he looked as if he would choke on the final word, '...goodwill.' Before the puzzled proprietor could question or protest, he added, 'I trust you received the previous sum I sent.' He glanced around. 'The place seems to be in...decent array again.'

'*You?*' the madam managed, her jaw agape.

'Don't sound so shocked,' he countered. 'I've funds enough to pay for my excesses.' He looked at her. 'After all, that's what it's all about, isn't it?' His eyes drilled into her soul. 'Money. All your kind understand money.' Here, he paid note to Heather. 'And I have *plenty*.' He turned back to the still-befuddled owner. 'So, have you a room?'

She shook her head as if to clear it, then seemed more like her normal self. 'Oh, of course, sir, right you are, then. We got several. Which do you fancy?'

'Your best, naturally,' he replied, with a mix of pleasure and impatience.

The madam was all business now, showing him to the finest room in the house of ill repute—after he had chosen his companion for the night, of course. This, as it turned out, fell to Heather, for she chanced to be the only one available at the time, and he opted not to wait. The madam left them at their room with a brief word to her customer about not being 'too rough on me girls or me furniture, if you please,' but both she and he knew it was an empty request; he had enough pounds on him to compensate for damage to either kind of property several times over, and it wasn't as if a brothel owner could go to the police. No, the most she could do was bar him access in future (assuming the doorman actually did his job), a measure he knew she'd not take unless things grew horrendous.

Thus it was that young Heather found herself in the poshest room of the tawdry little bordello...and in the company of this utterly frightening fellow. She said not a word, nor even made eye contact, but merely stood there as if awaiting instruction or punishment.

As it turned out, she got both.

'Damn it, girl, don't just stand there!' he commanded. 'Strip!'

She hurriedly complied, as if starting back into reality and trying to make up for the time lost to her unhappy daydreams.

Unfortunately, this was a bit too quick for her client's taste.

'Stupid strumpet!' he berated her. 'Don't do it so fast! I aim to get my money's worth.'

Doing her best not to quiver, she slowed her pace, though her hands still shook a trace as she unlaced her corset.

'Bloody lovely,' he pronounced as she shed the last of her apparel. 'That's more like it. Now,' he continued, the lust gleaming in his eye, 'do get on the bed.'

She did so, reclining as calmly as she could. She told herself this was just like any other job—nothing to it—that this man paid well and the madam would surely look upon her with favour if she pleased him and kept him (and his money) coming back for further pleasant experiences. She also knew her employer would be most displeased if she botched things up. And, more than that, Heather feared what her current client might do if she failed to meet his expectations.

'What do you fancy, sir?' she asked in this vein, propping herself up on her elbows as she did so. Having repositioned herself thusly, she turned her gaze to the man who was to have her.

He had already doffed his strange, black robe, which lay now in a dark, crumpled mass upon the burgundy-carpeted floor. This revealed to her his upper body, and she noticed that his build, though slight, was also wirily muscled. His chest, arms, and even abdomen were hirsute (not unlike someone whose ancestors came from a dry and sunny clime), the hair the same dark colour as the wavy locks that adorned his head and framed his pale yet dusky face. His eyes were very nearly black as his mane, and regarded her with a mixture of lust and unwholesome glee, as if she were a thing to be devoured.

'You,' he replied to her query. 'I fancy you very much, at the moment.'

And here, the young demimondaine noticed a change in the shape of his trousers, the only article of outer clothing he yet wore. Apparently, he fancied her quite a lot. Some men she serviced were embarrassed when this sort of thing happened so very quickly; others shrugged it off with a joke at their own expense, or complimented her on her tempting looks. Not so this fellow.

'Ah. There we are,' he stated, seemingly self-satisfied at the recent development, shedding his last garments the next instant. Heading toward her, he remarked, 'Of course, I doubt you're as good as Jeanine—or the twins—but you'll do.'

Heather took the comment in stride, having become used to worse insults than this in her past half-year as a whore. Besides, she was the least experienced of all the girls, a fact of which she was too well aware. When she'd first come here from the country, she'd known nothing, even quailing over positions she'd thought 'un-Christian.' She had been so naïve, an embarrassment to herself and her employer, who'd only just let her stay on after that incident with Dr Falstaff.

But now her present client approached her, clawing his way predatorily across the red satin sheets of the bed. In the next instant, his tongue invaded her mouth and his other part her inside. He went at her voraciously, feeling every part of her, his breathing heavy with instinctual lust. He took her with a passion deep and primal, as if he *needed* this to stay alive, not tiring till almost the break of dawn.

When the day came, Heather was much relieved, for never before had she had to serve a man so long, and he had been inordinately rough. When, at last, he had collapsed, out of pure exhaustion, still glorying in the pleasures he'd just known, his body weak and shuddering, soaked thoroughly with cooling sweat—when this had happened, he had almost immediately thereupon fallen asleep, his energies spent.

Seeing this, Heather let out a sigh of relief, grateful her service was finally over. After several minutes' recuperation, she shakily arose from the bed, her weakened muscles rendering it hard to walk, and put her clothes back on. She took stock of her body's condition as she did so: Her entire being was sore and weak, one breast and arm were bruised, her mouth felt raw, and she detected a slight bleeding in her nether region, thanks to the incessant pressure of her overeager client. This rendered her unusable for the next few nights. Even the madam let her rest during this time, for she knew well enough the taxing repercussions this man's ways had upon her girls. That was why she charged him significantly more than most; each wench he took was thereafter out of commission for a couple of days. She had learned this early on, back when he'd first started frequenting the place, and they'd come to an arrangement as to the fee. But then, one night, he'd become far too rough; Charlotte had perhaps displeased him in some way, and he'd laid into her. They and some patrons had chased him out then—or, rather, he'd fled—and the madam had feared the saucy French girl dead. She survived, as it turned out, but was never the same; from that night on, she'd had a look in her eye that couldn't be healed, as if part of her soul had been murdered. She'd run away back to Paris, not long after.

But it appeared to the madam that there wouldn't be a repeat this time around. She consoled herself that it had all probably been a great misunderstanding in the first place, that she hadn't made the ground rules of her brothel clear enough, that the man had simply lost his temper (as drunkards were wont to do) at Charlotte's tongue, that everyone had reacted much too quickly and with too much pride on every side involved.

Well, it seemed he had sincerely made up to her now. After all, there were plenty more bordellos in the city; he did not have to frequent hers, and yet he had sent her a great large sum, in effect fixing everything he had destroyed (except Charlotte, but that couldn't be helped), even after the tense incident with Dick Falstaff. Yes, she'd more than happily see to every want of her newest best customer, this unusual but quite well-off little imp. It was just good business, after all, and what patron didn't have his own small eccentricities…?

Yet she was cognisant of the toll his severe treatment took on her girls, and got young Heather a small glass of brandy to settle the poor thing's nerves after her ordeal.

'Thanks, mum,' Heather said, cradling the glass with cherishment and care.

'Figured you could use a nip,' the elder woman returned. ''S not every day that fellow comes callin'. 'E's one of our tougher customers, that one.' She glanced around. 'By the by, where is 'e?'

'Upstairs, sound asleep, last time I seen 'im,' Heather informed her, taking a swig to calm herself from what she'd been through.

'Good for all us lot, then,' the madam pronounced, casting a look of empathy in the weary girl's direction. 'Lord knows, 'e ain't the easiest bloke to endure.'

''E's 'ardly 'uman!' Heather declared, clutching her brandy as if fearful someone would come and steal it away. 'I swear, mum, 'e's more beast than man!' She looked down at her glass. 'I'm sorry,' she said simply, ashamed at her adamant outburst.

'I know we ought not speak ill of those what pays our bills, I know that, mum. But 'e...'e frightens me. I thought I'd made me way so far from when I first begun 'ere, thought I could 'andle what things most blokes threw at me, these days, but this one, mum...' She trailed off, gazing pitifully up at the madam through watery eyes, the tears threatening to drop. Her voice failed her as she found herself unable to continue.

'There, there, love,' her employer cooed reassuringly, placing a soft blanket round the shaken girl's slender shoulders. 'What say you get some rest now, poor thing? You did very well tonight, dear, very well. Let's find you a nice bed of your own now. And you can even lock the door, if it so please you.'

'Oh, yes, mum, thank you kindly!' Heather exclaimed with great relief. The madam then helped her on to bed, the tearful girl silently grateful for these small mercies.

'And don't you worry 'bout tomorrow night, miss,' the elder woman made clear. 'Just get your rest; a few days and you'll soon feel good as new. Meantime, I'll get the other girls to take your usual load. Sleep well, love.' And, with that, she left young Heather to herself.

The lass settled down, grateful to be within the warm embrace of pleasing, soft bedcovers all her own, instead of the rough grip of her last client.

CHAPTER EIGHTEEN

In another part of town, a recuperating, sore, indignant Richard Falstaff lay in bed, scared, seething, and uncomfortably stiff. He'd come altogether too close to being beaten to death; had his servants not arrived to chase his foul, deranged assailant away, he dreaded to think what fate might have befallen him. As it was, some rib bones (not to mention most of his flesh) were bruised, his left forearm was broken from his tumble out the window, and he had a cut on the right side of his head. It began just behind his ear and ran diagonally upward for some distance, terminating only where his temple met his forehead. The lower end of the gash was barely half an inch from a major ligament. He tried not to think on what would've happened had *that* been sliced. To come so close…it was almost as if the bugger had some knowledge of anatomy. Then again, he reasoned, the head and neck were the most obviously vulnerable parts of a man, especially if one attacked like a coward, from behind. It was likely pure dumb luck he'd almost wound up mortally wounding Dr Falstaff in this way. Still, that hadn't made the experience any less frightening. It had been so sudden, so ferocious—and in his own home! *That* was beyond the beyonds.

'I shall, of course, press charges,' Dick vowed aloud, though he was, at the moment, alone in his guest suite.

Daylight had come, and he felt safer now. (Being two storeys up, behind a guarded door, didn't hurt either.) In addition to the damage to his person, not to mention the violation of his home, it was the sheer audacity of the blighter and his subsequent attack that stuck in Dick's craw. After all, he was *Doctor Richard Falstaff*, esteemed man of medicine, a veritable pillar of society! Who was this lowly ruffian, to fancy he could trifle with such a man?

Come to think of it, he mused, *that was the same fool error our plague doctor made last night.* He chuckled as he thought of the royal arse the elder physician had made of himself, levelling ineffectual barbarities in the war of words he'd waged against his host.

'Tsk, tsk,' clucked Dick with satisfaction. 'Poor old Henry,' he chided with mock pity. 'I doubt anyone will have you over now.' He sighed, regretting that he'd not caught the doctor in time to expose his epilepsy to everyone there. *If only I could show them your overpowering mental weakness,* he thought. *Ah, well; I suppose your childish temper will have to suffice.* This word, 'temper', brought him back to his previous line of thought, reminding him, as it did, of the furious spirit of malice his masked attacker had exhibited when he'd tried to do in Falstaff that same night. *Why, Henry's display was naught but a little cloudburst, compared to* that *unruly tempest*, he observed. It seemed he had greater concerns right now than the ruining of one old doctor's reputation.

'Jenkins!' he bellowed, summoning one of his manservants.

'Yes, sir?' came a voice outside his room, just ere the ready, freckled face of Mr Jenkins peered around his master's door. Dick's doorguard was a lanky man, but strong, with a shock of ever-frizzy hair—ginger-hued, to match his fiery personality.

'Despatch one of the servants,' Dick ordered. 'Tell him to fetch someone from the police. And send another man to get my lawyer,' he added. With an evil gleam in his eye, he concluded, 'I should like to make a statement.'

***

Some hours later, the police had in their hands an account related them by none other than Dr Richard Falstaff himself (with some help from his attorney), describing the unwarranted brutalities committed upon his person—in his own home!—in the dead of night. The upstanding Londoner had been a little shaky in describing his assailant's physical characteristics, remembering in only hazy detail everything save his piercing eyes (though he did note the man's stature as being smaller than average). But the cruelties he had suffered, and the malevolent, frenzied manner in which they had been carried out, Falstaff recounted perfectly, showing the officers his wounded head in particular. His broken arm and some of the bruises, they could plainly see for themselves. Dick did not deign to rise from bed during the whole affair, citing that his injuries made the act unfeasible. (This was, however, not entirely true; though in pain, he really could get up whenever he desired. But there was no reason to let the police know that...)

The lawmen let the esteemed victim know that they would look into this matter right away.

'Don't you worry, Doctor Falstaff,' one assured. 'I'm sure we'll lay 'old of 'im before long. Meantime, Officer Cranston 'ere is ready to guard your person from future 'arm.'

The other bobby nodded his assent.

'Thank you, but that won't be necessary,' Dick informed them. 'As you can see, my man Jenkins here is quite capable, and I'd rather there be another officer out looking for the devil in the city, instead of in my home.'

'Very well, sir,' the first policeman noted. 'We'll get on that straight away.'

After they had left, Jenkins received an order from his master to send Mr Harberson, another servant, up to see the injured doctor. Shortly thereafter, Jenkins saw the other manservant depart the room and then the house. From what little he'd heard (not really by intent) through the guest door, it seemed Harberson was bound for some address in

Soho, of all places. Jenkins could not make heads or tails of the significance of all this talking, and so shrugged it off, excusing himself (once he'd made sure Dr Falstaff needed nothing more) to the kitchen for a bite. It wasn't his place to know, anyhow, and he was happy he had more than porridge to eat today.

'At least,' he consoled himself as he sat down to eat, 'I have chicken.'

CHAPTER NINETEEN

Later that same day, just after luncheon, John received a letter, which a messenger hand-delivered to his door. It came from Henry and read as follows:

Dear John,

> I trust you are well. It has come to my attention that you had an unwanted visitor in your domicile last night, for the fellow has told me so himself. It appears that, upon not finding me at home, he came to you for aid. He was apparently in quite a condition, likely having taken mind-altering substances, and I regret the troubles which resulted from his incursion. I know you do not like him, John, but I ask you not to judge him too harshly, for there is more to the story than last I told you. The short of it is, I owe my life to this fellow you so despise, whom everyone seems set on cornering and dragging to the gallows. (I do not desire to reveal under what

circumstances this transpired, as they could be called, at best, undignified.) I am, however, sure you realise what a debt this is, and hope this will at least partially illumine the reasons I have helped him, and continue to do so. Luckily, he has come to no harm as of yet, and I intend to keep it that way. I have provided him some funds and suggested a place to stay, though I know not whether he took this advice. He has also changed the name by which he goes (at least for the time being), having replaced it with a moniker of my own suggestion.

I am bound for warmer climes, in the hope the fresh air and sunshine will improve my health, which has been rather fickle as of late. I may be gone some time, but this is for the best.

If a Mr 'Harold Edwards' should come calling while I am thus out of reach, please, John, let the poor fellow in and do not hand him over to the law. I know you do not like him, but keep in mind, when next you set eyes on him (if such should come to pass), if you feel the wave of disgust rising up within you—again, I say, remember that this man is one who saved the life of your dear friend; and if that will not be enough to keep you from wanting to cast him out into the night or give him unto the cold, unforgiving, <u>strangling</u> arms of the law, keep in mind that your old friend Henry has asked you to give him succour—for the sake of our friendship, if nothing else. I doubt the need shall arise, for he (understandably) seems not to trust you with his welfare any longer, but should he find himself in desperate circumstances, I will feel the more secure knowing he has some person to whom he can turn.

There is a further thing I should like you to know: last night, when he came to you, 'Mr Edwards' meant you no harm. I fear he may have treated you a bit roughly, and I apologise for him, as he has to me. Truth be told, the fellow was simply scared for his life, and it was in this fearful desperation that he mistreated you thusly. Still, it was improper, and I do hope you can forgive him for it.

One last thing, John: It occurs to me you may have gone to speak with the police after the incident last night. If so, this is unfortunate, but I ask that you might try to mitigate the damage that may've been done. Mr Edwards would prefer that no one even knew of his existence, and is considering leaving the country as soon as he finishes what business he has left in London. I wonder if you might help in this matter, perhaps giving the police a description somewhat different from the way he truly looks. The thought has also just entered my mind that there was an attack perpetrated against Dr Richard Falstaff last night as well. (Though it was unfortunate, I cannot, in all honesty, say I am terribly sorry at this turn of events; you are, I'm sure, aware of Falstaff's character.) If he does decide to press charges, and if it should come to pass that Edwards is caught, I humbly request, for the sake of our old friendship, that you represent him at the trial which is sure to follow, and endeavour, if at all possible, to persuade those present that he has <u>no</u> <u>connection</u> <u>whatsoever</u> to the identity of that man who was found in my cabinet (for if anyone should realise they are one and the same, he shall hang for certain).

I know this all must seem rather strange to you, and I realise you are a man who would want all the reasons—and rightly so, I might add. Yet the time grows short, and I grow weary. Since I am unable to look after him, I pray that you will do so in my stead. Perhaps, one day, in better health, I can explain it all in a way so as to make you understand. For now, let what I have written here suffice. I remain,

Your ill but faithful friend,

And here John read his old chum's signature, his mind well full of wonder. What an odd letter, this! What strange requests—though, at least, Henry's explanation of what he owed this newly named Mr Edwards made things a little clearer. He pondered, with some puzzlement, when and how this Edwards could have saved his sick friend's life. But, in the end, he did as Henry'd asked. He told the police he'd remembered some details about the intruder he'd neglected the night before, giving them a visual description similar to but just different enough from what 'Harry Edwards' actually looked like. At the police station, he chanced to overhear that Richard Falstaff had given a (none-too-detailed) statement, so the attorney told the officers that he, too, had seen the violent man, letting his description supplement and colour Falstaff's own. In this way, he did his best to carry out Henry's requests—but for his friend's sake, not anyone else's. He still disliked the horrid little man.

***

Back at Dr Falstaff's, Dick, acutely aware that his door-guard Jenkins was still busy dining, had made his way back into the room of the assault. Searching over his bedroom (which the police were set to inspect the next day, due to a happenstance lack of manpower at present), Falstaff found the item he desired. It was a folded, yellowed piece of paper, lying unassumingly upon the hardwood floor, next to scattered fragments from the shattered porcelain vase. Dick picked it up, being careful not to disturb any other part of the scene as he did so. The document, he reasoned, had been too accessible, sitting in that vase. He dared not take the chance again of any of its contents coming to light. And yet he did not wish to burn the old piece of parchment; it served as a trophy of sorts, a reminder of his first and greatest victory to date, and thus held a kind of twisted sentimental attachment in his mind. To resolve this dilemma, he vowed to keep it on his person at all times, from that day forward. So deciding, he pocketed the thing, then went again to his guest room to put Jenkins back on watch.

CHAPTER TWENTY

Mr Bertram Harberson (called 'Bert' by anyone he counted as a friend) was a medium-sized man, as far as height was concerned, though he was stocky (and, truth be told, a tad pudgy) in build. He was in his mid-twenties and was a sensitive but jovial fellow, easy-going—even nonchalant—in day-to-day affairs, yet not without his own quiet concern. He worried after his friends (perhaps too much) and was his master's closest confidant.

Falstaff had recruited the chap from an orphanage over a decade ago, when Bert had been not quite thirteen and Dick had been just approaching thirty. Dick had seen the lad horribly abused by one of the older boys, and banked that he would be forever grateful to whosoever rescued him from such a situation. In this, he'd been correct. The doctor had taken Bertram to work in his house, and the boy had repaid Falstaff with his undying loyalty. Over the years, he had grown ever closer to Dick, who in turn eventually had felt comfortable enough around the servant to confide in him—and more. Thus it was that Dr Falstaff had today entrusted him to carry out an errand of great import, while Dick lay ineffectually in bed, injured and irked.

Harberson turned a corner and spied his intended destination. It was not really much to look at in the daylight, though he imagined business picked up swiftly after dusk. At present, however, no one seemed to be home—at least, so far as he could tell. The draperies were drawn, the lights were out, and he detected not a sound within. All these signs did not, however, dissuade him from his mission. He walked up to the entryway and rapped upon the door, most casually, in a pattern (as of music) Dick had described to him.

It took some minutes of waiting (along with repeated knocking on Bertram's part), but finally, his patience was rewarded. A gruff and groggy porter at last let Dick's servant in, though the suspicious doorman thought Bert's presence here was odd, particularly at this daylight hour. Still, all that was requested was a room and, as the madam was currently asleep, the porter gave this customer a key and pointed him toward his rented quarters. These happened to be on the upper floor, so Bertram started searching on this storey, believing it as good a place as any to begin. The brothel's surly doorman had fallen fast asleep not long after returning to his post. This meant that Harberson could freely survey the whole place without the slightest fear of being caught. And so he peeked through keyholes or (when unlocked) opened doors, taking account of whom (if anyone) each room contained. He chanced to spy several girls and women in this fashion, all of them asleep and only two within locked rooms. (One of these, he assumed, was the madam.) Some women he spied in only their nightclothes, or half-dressed, but these he did not linger on, for they did not concern him.

As Falstaff's man approached the end of one of the upper halls, he heard a set of footsteps of a most unusual character. They were light but definite, yet also highly erratic, as if their owner were a youthful man of strong will, possessed of frustrated or simply excessive energies (possibly both). This portrait of the man, in fact, proved true, as Harberson discovered when he peered through the locked keyhole of the door to the bordello's finest room.

The occupant could be no older than his early to mid-twenties. He was pacing in an anxious, random way, clearly on edge, with not a little anger in his gait. The rolled-up legs of overly long, loose trousers (the waist of which was held up by a belt) flapped to and fro with every sudden step their owner took. His coal-black hair, made darker still by its contrast to his pale and sickly skin, impacted his bare shoulders as he went, though he seemed not to notice as he paced unevenly about the room. Once, he stopped before a nightstand, over which a jet-black garment lay. He looked at it a moment; then, with a snarl of bestial frustration, he gave the whole affair a sudden kick, toppling robe and table to the floor.

Bertram stared, entranced. The whole thing had the feel of some great train wreck; he gawked in fascination and disgust. There was something about this odd, unseemly little fellow, pacing about in those regrettable trousers, anger shot through all his features, committing violence upon the furniture—there was something at once laughable, unsettling, and sad in all of this, and the voyeur could not help but sigh, not realising he did so till too late.

The man he had been watching stopped dead cold. His startled look bespoke both fear and ire, like an animal smelling a trap. Harberson blanched as his intended quarry crossed the room, stalking his way, barefooted, towards the door, his top lip curled upward in a snarl. His eyes exuded only fear and hate—feral, but with a cagey human intellect beneath. The worst aspects of beast and man beaconed from this cruel visage, an outer warning of the soul inside.

Bertram saw the hall, the steps, the portal in a blur, rushed past the porter, fled into the street and down the block, not stopping till he found himself upon his master's doorstep, red-faced from his exertion, banging in a panic on the solid cherry wood. It was not until he was admitted entrance, and had a shot of whiskey for his nerves, that he calmed down enough to come to his senses. He realised he had run out of the brothel straight away, not thinking where he went till he was home, safe, in his master's house, his refuge. He shook his head to clear it, but could not. He'd witnessed something he should not have seen, should never have seen—a blasphemy that shouldn't have existed, and yet *did*. He had no words to describe it, but it scared him to his core, unto his soul; it threatened to bring his faith to its knees—he could not bear it! He begged his master, for whom he'd thought he would do *anything*, not to send him out to search for this man (if, indeed, a man he could be called) ever again. Dick gave him this small respite, satisfied that he knew where his assailant had been hiding.

He informed Scotland Yard that very day.

CHAPTER TWENTY-ONE

Back in the bordello, 'Mr Edwards' cursed. He'd caught a glimpse of someone fleeing out the door, a man (if memory served him) he'd seen once at Falstaff's, a servant of the doctor's, whose name he hadn't learned.

'Damnation!' he swore aloud from the top of the stairs, looking down at the still-swinging door Falstaff's lackey had used in his escape. The porter stood beside it, sleepy and bewildered. 'Don't just stand there, man!' Edwards commanded him. 'Rouse your mistress!'

The doorman left immediately to go wake the one to whom all answered. The madam arrived shortly, looking half-asleep. Edwards, still half-dressed, had by this time made his way downstairs, and now stood impatiently, leaning against the bar, his fingers drumming the smooth countertop.

'What's the trouble, then?' the owner asked, not pleased at having been awakened thusly, but also worried something might be amiss.

'Falstaff's found us,' her new best customer declared, his drumming fingers drawing to a fist. 'He'll no doubt send the peelers here post haste.'

'Peelers? Why the bloody 'ell would Doc Dick want to lead the police 'ere? It's been ages since last 'e paid us any visit; I thought we'd never see the chap again. What's 'is quarrel with us?'

'With me,' her patron answered. 'His quarrel is with me, though doubtless he cares not a whit if you go down as well. Arrogant cad.'

'What trouble 'ave you brought upon me 'ouse, man?!' cried the madam. 'I can't afford to 'ave the peelers 'ere! Why, it would ruin me! What do y—?'

'Be *silent*!' he barked, pounding his fist upon the counter in rage, his eyes forming the wickedest glare.

The madam swore he seemed as if he wanted to choke the life out of her—literally—squeeze her larynx until she couldn't make a sound and all the breath had left her lifeless body. She had a sudden, visceral image of this horror in her head, which stopped her tirade, stillborn, in its tracks. The porter took a step toward him as if to come to the madam's defence and eject him. Edwards shot him a look so black and so eager for murder that the doorman thought better of it and simply turned away sheepishly.

'Now,' Edwards continued, seemingly coming back to himself from the very edge of aggression, 'I suggest you find yourself and all your girls someplace to go. *Quickly*. Bobbies are slow, but not in the physical sense.'

'Suppose we all get out, sir,' the porter ventured obsequiously. 'What good'll it do?

They'll probably 'ave this entire block on watch, they will. Where are we to 'ide, then?'

'I do not care,' retorted the rogue. With an air of condescension, he concluded, 'Though your thinking in this matter is skewed from lack of wits.' The doorman was offended, but he dared not interrupt. 'What will the police do, I wonder,' the reprobate asked, 'when they find a whorehouse with no occupants? The most that they can do is search the place, which benefits them nothing if they fail to find their man, or even a stray strumpet to haul in. And suppose they should then search all through the neighbourhood, as you suggest. This is Soho, my feeble-minded friend. The bumbling bobbies have no way to tell one fallen woman from another; all of the girls could easily blend in at any other brothel on this block, with the peelers none the wiser. You, in fact,' he suggested, turning now toward the madam, 'could even set up shop some other place—temporarily, of course, just until the lawmen leave (which, believe me, they inevitably will)—and all for a small cut to whoever owns the place you choose to stay. They are *your* girls, madam, and better than most of the rubbish you find around here. People will seek them out, I have no doubt.' Here he looked to her with an air of satisfaction, then threw the porter an exasperated glance, as if to call him a moronic git. 'I trust you're *satisfied?*' he asked rhetorically, to which the doorman merely nodded, ashamed at his own being dense.

Assumptions

The madam seemed pleased enough, given the circumstances.

'Blimey,' she exhaled, relieved the police couldn't stop her business after all. 'Right, then. Off we go. Pritchard!' she commanded the porter. 'Rouse everyone 'ere immediately! We 'ave to get to Gretchen's straight away!' (This was another house of ill repute, down the street.)

'Right, madam.' Mr Pritchard obeyed her. He moved off down a hallway, opening each door he came to, awakening the occupants within.

The madam soon set out to do the selfsame thing, but not before she spoke with the strange man who'd just doomed, then saved, her livelihood.

'You got a place to get to, Eddie?' she asked him, not wanting her top customer to get himself in jail.

'I believe so. By the by, it's "Edwards" now. "Mr Harold Edwards". And you'd never seen me before that summer night—the night that bugger Falstaff started this bloody feud!' His face was pure malevolence as he thought of the man.

'Alright then. As you will, "Mr Edwards". Now we'd better get ourselves gone, the both of us.'

'Indeed.'

He fetched the rest of his clothes from upstairs, then took his leave. The madam got her girls out in time, too, everyone and Mr Pritchard heading down to Gretchen's, where the madam promptly worked out an arrangement.

The police, as predicted, did not really know what to make of the ghostly bordello, the curtains drawn, the liquor carried away. As also foreseen by Mr Edwards, they did indeed post men along the street, not paying any mind to other brothels on the block—in truth, the most that happened was that some officers chose to patronise such places when off duty. Never did they notice that the number of harlots had increased at one of these establishments, or that the overall quality of the girls at Gretchen's had, somehow, mysteriously improved.

Of their true quarry, the dastardly assailant of Dick Falstaff, the lawmen could find not the slightest trace.

CHAPTER TWENTY-TWO

The same day as Bertram Harberson's frightful foray into one of Soho's shady brothels, Henry's friend, John, heard a fitful knock upon his door, round about four o'clock in the afternoon. As he happened to be walking 'cross the foyer, he answered it himself.

The face that greeted him was not a pleasant one. The man was hurried, worried, rueful, frantic.

'Did you get it?' he asked John warily, close to panic, looking as if he might flee any instant.

John regarded him a moment, the shock of his appearance here causing the lawyer to hesitate.

'Did you get the letter, John?!' the unexpected fellow asked him again, desperation patent in his tone.

'Ah. Yes,' said the attorney finally, causing his visitor's anxiety to subside—or, at least, to lessen enough so as not to be overly noticeable. 'Do come in,' John forced himself to say.

Edwards nearly leapt across the threshold, impatient for the door to close behind him.

'I'm glad you received it,' the smaller man managed, trying his utmost to be calm, but tremulous with excited energy nevertheless.

John, having locked the door, thought, *Yes. I'll bet*, but outwardly tried to hide his distaste, reminding himself that he did this for Henry, who somehow owed his life to this strange devil.

'I think it should be wise if we withdrew,' the lawyer stated. 'I assume you will explain to me the reasons behind your present arrival at my home.'

'Naturally,' Edwards responded, scoffing at the idea that John would even think that he might not. 'I'll let you in on every gory detail, if you so desire.'

'I don't know that that will be necessary. But come, let us withdraw.' John bade him enter the drawing room, making sure the madman went in first. He wasn't about to turn his back on him.

The lawyer's guest settled into a chair with much relief, visibly relaxing when John bolted shut the door so that no errant servant would disturb them.

'So, then,' John began, taking a seat, 'I am to call you "Harold Edwards", I presume?'

'If it suits your fancy,' replied his visitor nonchalantly. 'Though you may address me by my other name, if no one else can hear us.'

'Very well, then,' John returned. 'So, Miste—'

'No, no, no, John! That won't do at all.' He tsked the old attorney. 'There really is no need to be so formal. After all, we've met before, you and I. And we have a mutual friend in dear old Henry.'

'Fine, then,' uttered John. 'I do not care what name you choose to go by.' He gazed at his unpleasant, smirking guest, wishing he would leave his abode now. 'I think that there is something you should know,' the lawyer informed him.

'Oh?'

'Whatever we may discuss here today, whatever I may do on your behalf in future, know that it is for the sake of Henry, out of honour for my oldest friend, that I do anything that may benefit *you*. To be honest, I despise you, Edward. If I had my way, I'd see you hanged before the morrow. I shall not pretend to like you in the least.'

'Fair enough,' the other countered, 'though you cannot know the details, so you really shouldn't judge. And don't pretend *you've* never sinned before. Even if you haven't done a wrong thing in your life—which I very much doubt—don't tell me that you've never thought, just once, of doing things society forbade. Don't tell me you've never felt that sinking feeling in the pit of your stomach when you round a corner and run into a bobby, even if it isn't you he's after. Everyone's done something rather less than good, John, or at the least, has entertained the thought. Don't preach to me from your great, high horse. We're more alike than you'd care to admit.'

The lawyer sighed.

'I have not acted on so many thoughts as you,' John clarified, 'though I concede your main point is well taken, if a trifle obvious.

Why, every man alive faces temptation—that is a fact I shall not dispute. Yet still there is gradation in the scheme. Surely, even you must admit, there is a great deal of difference in the conduct of one considered a saint and in the actions of a *murderer.*' Here he looked pointedly at Edward.

'Do you consider your friend Henry a saint?' his houseguest asked. 'If you found out the contrary, would you still stay by his side? Or would you throw him to the wolves, as you did me?'

'I am aware Henry is not a saint,' John informed him, quietly annoyed. 'You are proof enough of that.'

At this, the hunted fugitive gave a rueful laugh, as if something were funny just to him, and yet quite sad.

'*I* am proof enough?' he echoed. 'You mean to say, my mere association with your friend is enough paltry evidence to fell him from his mighty pedestal?' He chortled. 'Am I so wicked, and your friendship so weak?'

'Not at all, to the latter,' John asserted, a mite offended, 'though I concur you are a wicked man. No, what I meant is that Henry, in his letter, explained to me that the circumstances under which you saved his life were, as he put it, "undignified". I can only imagine what he meant by that and how you figure in, but it matters not. He is my friend, and nothing he could do will ever change that.'

'Nothing?' queried Edward, torn between suspicion and incredulity.

'Nothing,' John reaffirmed.

'What if he had killed a man, as I have?'

'He would not. But even if he had, I know Henry, and I'm certain that he would have had his reasons.'

'But what if he had murdered someone savagely, John? What if he had lost all sense of mind and tasted sweet delight from every blood-drenched blow?'

'You mean, as you did?' The lawyer scowled.

'Yes, just as I did.' Edward smiled.

'He would not.'

'You do not know your friend.'

'Nonsense. He is a reasonable man, and I've known him for over forty years—longer than you have yet lived, no doubt. And though Harry has, in private, expressed to me a certain dislike of some of society's practices, he nonetheless adheres to them...as must we all. I daresay he's the most civilised man I've ever met. What's more, I have never known him to be so judgemental as to truly hate another man.'

'What of Hastie?'

'How do you—?' John started to ask, then remembered that Henry had told this blighter many things, probably including his past tiff with their friend, Hastie. 'That is another matter,' the lawyer stated.

'How? Didn't he despise the narrow-minded fool?'

'I do not know how you could so misinterpret Henry,' John declared. 'He disagreed with

Hastie, yes, because Henry held true to his beliefs regarding medicine's potential, while Hastie saw him as impractical—if I understand the situation correctly. Even when they had their falling out, however, it was merely over each other's positions—a move to agree they disagreed—not malice toward the view-holder himself.' Here he gazed pointedly at his guest. 'A case of "Hate the sin and love the sinner", I suppose, on both their parts. But what of it?' John looked downward. 'Hastie is gone now. And Harry's health is fickle, as of late,' he continued, solemnly, staring at his lap. 'I do not have that many friends left, Edward,' he said sadly, half to himself. Still without glancing up, he concluded, with sincerity and conviction, 'I would do anything for those that yet remain to me. *Anything.* My aiding *you* is proof enough of that.' And here he raised his head up wearily to regard the man who faced him, expecting to see that infuriating smirk of his, that look of satisfaction and conceit.

Instead, the lawyer did a double-take. Edward's entire expression had changed. He looked like a different man. His countenance, normally so off-putting, was (John realised) rendered so only by his demeanour—which, as of now, had almost wholly altered. Instead of smugness, anger, hate, or fear, the astounded attorney noticed tears in the man's eyes, his jaw aquiver, an air of—what was it? Joy? Relief? Contrition? Gratitude?—imbued throughout his being.

Thank you, John, was all the man could think, a surge of sweet elation—coupled with humility and thankfulness—welling up within his soul. With this transmutation of his inner, ethereal core, another change began to manifest.

John looked on, full of fear and morbid wonder, as the small man before him began trembling through and through, doubled over in the chair in pain, emitting a sound between a cry of agony and an ecstatic laugh, then swelled in size, his features melding, complexion altering, hair changing its hue and length. All the while, a horrid, grinding sound, as of bones and tendons grating—*growing*—filled John's ears, until, at last, his houseguest stopped this strange, lurid display, and sat there, pale and shaky, panting as if starved for breath, the perspiration glistening on his fine and handsome brow. He gazed up at the lawyer through clear green eyes, his short, dark-brown hair tousled, hands upon his knees to lend support even while sitting.

'John,' he gasped, as soon as he was able. The attorney sat there, thunderstruck. 'Oh, John, thank God for you!' he managed, still struggling for every grateful breath. 'I...don't know...what I...would've done—'

'*Henry?!*' his friend half-gasped, half-cried, starting from his seat as if possessed.

'Yes. Yes, John, 'tis...I. I tried to...tell you, before, John, remember? The drugs—you insisted,' he explained, his breathing a little less laboured now. 'You insisted it was the drugs, that I'd been hallucinating, out of my mind, when I told you everything that'd transpired. It was true, John—everything I told you—the absolute truth, ludicrous and pitiable as it is. But it's true, every bit of it, the case statement—my confession—everything! Here,' he said, rising, holding out his hands, 'see for yourself.'

John was not sure what to do. He saw his old, dear, frightening, compassionate, hateful, grateful friend; he touched the doctor's hands and face as in a dream, his rational mind refusing to believe the truth his fingers felt and eyes reported back to his baffled brain.

Then, as if awakening, the attorney snapped back to himself, his logical but pattern-seeking mind putting all the pieces into place, against his will, almost against *itself*. What had been improbable, *impossible*...was *true*.

CHAPTER TWENTY-THREE

'What a mess!' John declared. 'What a terrible mess!'

'I know,' Henry confided. 'But you have saved me, John! You have brought me back from the very brink of my destruction!'

'For how long?' countered the doctor's longtime friend. 'You said in your confession the change could come on you without a moment's notice. How long before the law hunts you again? Before you turn into... *that*?'

'I don't know, John. But, listen, it's not exactly as it was. I think there must have been some sort of alteration—a chemical or alchemical reaction, within my personal physiology—when I ingested the cyanide before you broke down the door.'

'What do you mean?'

'I am unsure precisely how it happened, chemically speaking—you know from my case statement that I never could identify what the impurity in the original salt was that made the whole damnable enterprise work in the first place.'

The lawyer nodded.

'Yet I have noticed,' the man of medicine continued, 'that since my "death" the changes have become less frequent.'

'Chang_es_? You mean to say you've turned and then come back to yourself on your own? Before our current conversation?'

'Precisely.'

'But, then,' John reasoned, trying to fit the problem to his mind, 'you would have had to change one time again, for—'

'Yes, John,' his friend interrupted, shame-faced. 'I am aware of the condition in which I showed up at your door. Yes, it has happened twice—forth and back, twice.'

'Surely, after the first time, Harry, you would have thought to count your blessings then. Why tempt fate a second time—or, if you have any control over these changes, since you say your situation is now different, why stay in that horrid, hateful form? Why not aim to be yourself again?'

'Don't you think I tried?!' the doctor's voice rose. 'Good God, John, do you think I *wanted* to stay *that*? It's horrible! The tension, the boiling, baseless anger, being hunted everywhere I turned, unable to trust a soul, even my dearest friend, unless I wrote him a letter in my handwriting soliciting him on my own behalf, calling on the sake of our old friendship—all this, just so that a just, patient, honourable man, a man I've counted as my friend since boyhood, would show the smallest mercy to my odd and hateful frame and not leave it to dangle on the gallows! Good God, John! Who would *want* to be that way?!'

John was silent, thinking only, *Well, you* must *have wanted to, at some point, else you would not have tinkered with such transcendental matters.* Yet these were not words fit for a friend—an ill and tortured friend, especially—and so the lawyer kept them to himself.

'Then how does it happen?' John asked simply.

'It's a trifle hard to—that is, I have a theory, but... You do remember the confession I wrote, John?'

'Naturally.'

'And do you also recall the part therein, wherein I recounted my experience at the Regent's Park?'

'Yes, to an extent. Perhaps you should refresh my memory, though, if it ties into this "theory" of yours.'

'Very well. There is a passage—I recall not how precisely I have worded it—referring to my thoughts upon my neighbours—other upstanding Londoners, you must understand.'

'Of course.'

'There was a moment in my flow of thoughts, as I sat upon that park bench, contemplating the people within our circles—there was a moment when I thought of their hypocrisy, and justified my actions in that I was like my neighbours.'

'Ah, yes,' John remembered. 'I do recall reading that section. Are you saying that this thought, that you and everyone were hypocrites, is what triggered the change in you that day?'

'No, John.' Henry sighed. 'I think upon that moment more than enough. No, it was not any sort of "pass" of being like my neighbours that was the catalyst. No, indeed, that could not be the case, for, even though it seems an excuse—which, I do not deny, it somewhat was—that thought contained within it also notes of shame. For certainly, you know how much I loathe hypocrisy. This was, then, also an indictment of myself. No, it took a much more arrogant thought than "I am like my neighbours" to damn my soul.'

'Go on.' John thought he might know where all this was headed, but didn't want to colour Henry's views. 'What was it?'

'"I am better than my neighbours—I am good, while they are bad. I labour for the benefit of greater humankind, while they, by their mere laziness, are cruel." Think of it, John.'

'But you do have a point,' the lawyer countered. 'You *do* see to the sick, the poor. They do not. You give freely of your time. They do not.'

'That is beside the point!' the doctor cried. 'John, for God's sake, *think* of it! This was after they had found Sir Danvers Carew! After I had... Oh, God.' He couldn't continue. His voice choked, his eyes awash with tears that threatened to spill over. He sat and buried his face deep in his hands, unable to look his old friend in the eye.

'You read it, John,' he said at last, his voice raw and ragged. 'You know what I did.

You even gave me the cane with which I—God help me...'

He made for a most pitiable, tragic sight, thought John. The look in Henry's eye didn't bode well; he seemed fit to be swallowed by his sadness.

'Harry,' said the lawyer, reaching over and strongly drawing his chum's chin up with one hand. 'You will keep a stiff upper lip. What's done is done, and cannot be changed. You are my friend. You have survived this long. You will go forward. And throw out any poisons you may have.' He'd be damned if he'd lose another friend to despair of any kind. 'I never knew until reading your confession how seriously you'd considered self-slaughter. I declare to you, from this day forth, you shall *never* contemplate that damnable, cowardly act, or I shall hold you personally responsible for the death of the last dear friend, outside my family, who yet remains to me! You have been given a life and, what's more, a second chance. I shall not tolerate it if you waste these!'

Having said his piece, John settled back into his seat. Henry was shocked, awed, and a mite afraid...but also joyful.

'Well?' asked John. 'What say you?'

Harry gave a wan smile. 'As you wish.'

CHAPTER TWENTY-FOUR

'Now tell me about the method,' John began, referring to when Henry had his fits. 'How does it come about, on each occasion?'

'Well, as I was saying earlier,' the doctor told him, 'I've noticed that the…"change for the worse", shall we say, occurs when I've a particular tone of thought.'

'And what is that?'

'I'm not exactly sure how to describe it. It's a sense of…of arrogance, self-righteousness. The feeling of being better than someone and right in thinking so. A bit like entitlement, I suppose—but with no regard for others or, worse, a disdain—even a hatred—of them.'

'Ah. That's what must have happened when you had your talk with Falstaff in the… house of ill repute.'

'Yes. Well, he had made a proper arse of himself—which, granted, is not all that out of the ordinary, for him. But then he made such comments, referring to the widow Denman and Ginny—two very kind-hearted people, you understand; they took me in when I had nowhere to go—'

'Yes, yes, I am aware,' John reassured him, then tried to get the doctor back on track. 'But what was it precisely about Dr Falstaff—what was it he said that was the catalyst for the thought process which you so described?'

'It was,' here Henry clenched his teeth, and then his fist, 'an unkind comment that he made about young Ginny. The girl is only ten—well, she was at the time; I imagine she's fast approaching eleven now—but as I've said, she is only a child, and not the cruel or bratty kind at that—in fact, far from it! At any rate, Falstaff informed me, in no uncertain terms, that this little girl, whom life has so mistreated, and who remains a flower despite it—he told me that he hoped to see her sold into a life of prostitution! That he would take great pleasure out of it, out of *her*! It was appalling!'

'Harry,' said John, playing Devil's advocate, 'in all fairness, you frequent houses, too.'

Henry sighed, his fist and teeth unclenching as he slumped into his chair.

'I know,' he said, looking at the ground. 'I know. I would have stopped by now, John, if I could. God knows I've tried.' He sighed again, turning toward his friend. 'Why do you think I started my experiments? Though I'd aimed for a clean divide, I had no care which way I ended up, to be honest—wholly good, wholly evil. I was willing to take the chance if it meant any relief from the unremitting, daily torture of my accursed, conflicted state. I didn't even care that all the chemicals might kill me. I simply could not go on the way I was. It was too painful. And yet, here I am.' He glanced about, then noticed the look on his friend's face. 'You needn't worry, John. I made you a promise. I may not be able to keep any made to myself, or even to God, but I shall honour those I make to you. You have my word.'

John nodded his approval.

'Very good,' noted the attorney.

Things were going better, now. He had fully recovered from the shock of witnessing his friend's transformation (though he still replayed it visually in his mind's eye with wonder), and aimed to put Henry's self-inflicted ailment under control. The first step to that was to categorise and understand it. The doctor had explained to John all his physical symptoms—in medical terminology, no less, though the lawyer had had to ask for layman's terms to some of them. Now the shrewd solicitor had shifted his focus to the actual trigger for change: the 'thought patterns', as Harry had referred to them.

'Suppose you might describe the temper of your thoughts when Dr Falstaff said what he did about that girl, as well as the actual words or images of these, if you can recall them.'

'Let's see...' Henry said, glancing sideways as he tried to find the words. 'I became rather put out with him, understandably. I remember thinking or feeling something along the lines of "That's not right!" or "How dare he?!" I was angry, but there was something more than that.' He thought a moment. 'Ah, yes,' he said, remembering. His cheeks and ears turned pink, and he looked down at the floor, ashamed of himself.

'What was it?' prompted the lawyer.

Henry looked at him, self-loathing dominant upon his face, but with just a wisp of pride showing about his slyish eyes. He recounted ruefully, 'I thought of his cruelty, his arrogance, the depths to which he would descend to hurt other people out of pure spite. And I thought so lowly of him, in that instant, that I felt myself to be leagues higher than he...even in my worst of moments. Then that worst of moments came upon me, and I proved myself wrong.'

'I see,' said John. 'What about the other time since then?'

Henry chuckled sadly. 'Dick Falstaff again, unfortunately.'

'Really?' his old friend queried, with a curious half-smile.

Henry nodded.

'Well, it seems that you and Falstaff just don't mix,' the attorney observed.

'To say the least. I tell you, John, he is the most infuriating man I've ever met.'

'Hm. That's saying a lot, Henry. I've known you longer than anyone; you're not the type to make waves over nothing.'

'The man is a fraud,' the physician explained. 'He has so many people fooled: they think he's a decent fellow. I know better, but I cannot make anyone else see past his façade. The only other person who seems to rain on his charade is Cedric Crespin—the banker—'

'I met him once,' John interjected. 'Decent enough fellow. Boisterous, but decent for all that.'

'Yes, my sentiments exactly,' put in Henry. 'What I was getting at, however, is how easily Falstaff fools those who don't know him well—and even some who do, I should imagine.'

'All very interesting, Harry,' agreed John, 'but, for the moment, let us concentrate on your condition and a way it might be managed.'

'I don't know that such a thing can be done.' The doctor shook his head. 'It seems as uncontrollable as the tide.'

'Yet the moon controls the tide,' countered the lawyer.

'What has that to do with me?' asked Henry.

'Why, my friend, you must become the moon as well as the tide. It is not impossible. Your sitting here before me, quite yourself, is proof enough. We need only to understand the process's workings.'

Henry thought a moment.

'You are right, John,' he said suddenly, his head snapping up, eyes wide and bright, as if he'd just latched on to some idea, the key that would decode his change in states. 'When I fell into that worse way of being, both times, it was preceded by a lack of empathy, a most unpitying view of Dr Falstaff as a *thing* to be despised—much worse than I—an entity without a shred of any redeeming quality whatsoever. He turned, for me, from a person to an object—and an unnecessary, offensive object, at that. Whereas,' he continued, 'both times I returned to my normal self, it was upon experiencing the opposite emotions. For instance, when I learned that Richard's "uncle", Dr Denman—when I learned what he had done, learned that Falstaff, though I hated him, had also suffered...in that instant, he became human again. And, thus, so did I. This was not enough to keep him from making an arse of himself and a fiend of me when we met most recently, however, as he rendered himself inhuman—and I felt myself justified and superior in comparison—once again. And, just here, today, when you were speaking of me, to me, as your friend—your true friend—you showed yourself to be the truest friend of all. This action swept me out of that harsh state. It is difficult to explain, John, but when my mind is like that, it is as if I care for no one at all, save myself. Or if I do, the feeling is ignored, sometimes purposefully overridden. This is easy enough to do, in that frame of mind.

'But you have done it, John!' he cried, standing up. 'You broke through, whether you meant to or no. It is the only reason I am here, as you now see me, able to talk to you about these matters, my mind unclouded, to realise my own malady's cause and cure. John, this is superb! We have done it! In a psychological, potentially unprovable way, I do admit, but here it is! Thank God!' He sat down again, relieved. 'Thank God. I was afraid...' He trailed off, then decided to say the words aloud, just to get them out of his heart: 'I was afraid it could've gone like those months past—when I feared to go outside, lest the change take me, not able to drink in the chill of the air or even fall asleep without suddenly reverting to that most unpleasant form.' He looked downward. 'That was a miserable time, to say the least.'

'It's in the past now, Harry. There's no need to dwell on it. The present is here, the future awaits, and you're a good sight better off than you were before, despite the fantastic events you have endured.'

'You're right, of course,' said Henry with a smile. 'Thank you, John.'

The lawyer merely shrugged.

'What are chums for?'

CHAPTER TWENTY-FIVE

Weeks passed, and found Henry in better spirits. John's talk with him had bolstered his resolve; he now found it easier to get through each new day, vowing he'd yet master his condition. After all, Man was a being of free will, was he not? It therefore might not prove impossible. To this end, he took to deep reflection, imagining Dick Falstaff in his mind. When waves of hatred arose in response, he endeavoured to transmute them into a calm, sad sea of empathy—or pity, at the least. He thought on Dick's suffering (though a part of him wondered if perhaps Dick had enjoyed the time spent with his 'uncle'), constructing in his head sombre vignettes, wherein a younger Falstaff—still a student, not yet a doctor—was preyed upon, felt fearful, could do nothing to deflect Denman's advances. He tried to know the shame Dick must have felt, the loathing for himself and for the famous doctor, over whom he'd had no power at all.

It must have been a terrible position, Harry concluded. *No doubt the man was utterly miserable. Trapped, powerless, ashamed, and full of fear... Small wonder, then, he's turned out as he has. A saint would be hard-*

pressed to do things any differently, to see the world as anything but foul—and return the favour, I suppose.

So moved was he—profoundly moved—that he thought of seeing Falstaff straight away, to let Dick know that he bore him no ill, but rather sympathy for the younger fellow's plight.

Perhaps, Henry reflected, *this action will prove to his benefit. It may even set off a realisation like my own, when John stood by me. I doubt that Dr Falstaff has ever known anyone whom he could fully trust, around whom he felt safe and truly wanted. If this unhappy fact can change, why, then, perchance the chap will finally be free—free to live his life, no more a slave to bitterness and the misery of spite.*

So inspired, Harry promptly dressed to go out, a servant readying his hat and cape—along with his new walking stick, of course. This done, the dapper doctor strode optimistically out the door, whistling a little as he went, headed for his prior enemy's overly gaudy abode.

***

Upon arriving at Falstaff's home, Henry knocked upon the heavy door and was soon greeted by a manservant of Dick's—the very one he'd seen fleeing the brothel in Soho. Momentarily surprised, the doctor lost his words and, with a brief, irrational thrill of terror, feared the man would run for the police.

'May I help you, sir?' asked Harberson, when the gent upon the doorstep had said nothing. Looking at him, Bertram thought this bloke looked vaguely familiar. Hadn't he been at one of the master's parties...?

Harry came back to himself at the servant's query.

'Ah. Yes,' he said, shifting his cane to his other hand. Introducing himself, he informed Mr Harberson that he'd come to pay a visit to Dr Falstaff, whereupon Bert asked if Henry would kindly wait a moment while he went to ask his master if he would see anyone. This question, as it turned out, was answered in quite the affirmative; when Dick learned what man stood at the door, he ordered him let in at once and shown the utmost hospitality. This, Bertram did, explaining that Dr Falstaff would be down presently; Dick wasn't yet fully dressed for company.

***

Henry sat in an ornate chair, considering how best he might begin with Dr Falstaff. He knew the tone of what he wanted to say but was having trouble finding which particular words he should employ. His intent was admirable, of that there was no doubt, but the phrasing had to be most delicate. A man possessed of such pride and suspicion as Dick would not be easily won over; he would require a very careful finessing, as his natural inclination was to think the worst of anything Henry said.

Yet, Harry thought to himself, *I must try to comfort him nevertheless. This was an act of kindness shown to me, and led to my salvation. I cannot knowingly leave this soul-scarred fellow, malicious as his words to me may've been, in such a wretched, pitiable state.*

***

Falstaff, meanwhile, had his own agenda. He did not know to what he owed this unexpected visit from the senior physician, but he was not about to let the moment pass him by, despite his suspicions.

As a matter of fact, Dick reasoned, *this presents the perfect opportunity for me to ferret out his darkest secrets. At the very least, I shall attempt to discern his connection with that treacherous, villainous devil who found me of late.* For Falstaff suspected that the scoundrel might have attacked him on Henry's behalf. *It is not improbable, given that the two men seem to be of intimate relation. Why, I'll bet he put the hateful bravo up to it. The knave did, after all, address me regarding matters of concern to the old fool: the welfare of Uncle Harry's witch of a widow and that abominably cheerful little child—the Devil take the both of them.* His hand moved to his waistcoat pocket unconsciously, as if to check whether its contents were still there. Falstaff had been frustrated, these past few weeks; the lawmen whom he'd tipped off had failed to find the fast-fled fugitive. Now Henry'd come to give Dick one more chance.

'Wherever he may be, I'll flush him out,' said Falstaff to himself. 'He shall not escape his just due.' So vowing, he descended the dark stairs that led to where his prey sat, unsuspecting.

CHAPTER TWENTY-SIX

The hairs on the back of Henry's neck stood up. He had a sudden feeling of alarm, though he saw no rational reason why. Just after this, he heard the sound of footfall coming down the steps, drawing closer to the cramped and narrow sitting room where he now found himself.

Falstaff entered. Henry felt a wave of unthinking hatred rise up inside him the moment he laid eyes on the man. However, he soon forced it down, drowning it out with images of how Dick must have suffered, reminding himself he was here to help this fellow, not despise him.

'Doctor Falstaff,' Henry stated, rising from his seat. 'You startled me.'

'Oh?' asked Dick, rather less than innocently. 'So terribly sorry. Though you do seem a bit jumpy, my dear doctor,' he remarked, locking the door to ensure no one would interrupt them.

'It is nothing,' returned Henry, shaking his head as if to cast off troubling thoughts. 'I trust you are well?'

'Are you joking, doctor?' Falstaff said with bitterness. He looked down at his injured arm, still bound within its sling.

'I meant, under the circumstances, are you faring as well as can be expected?' the elder gentleman clarified apologetically.

'I suppose. Why? Did you think I'd been "done in", as some folk term it?' He shot his guest an accusatory glare.

'Why, no. No, not at all,' Henry stated, the images from his vicious attack on the now-injured man instantly replaying in his mind. He felt suddenly weak, a trifle ill, and sank meekly into the nearby sofa.

'Problems, doctor?' Dick asked with a note of subtle menace as he sat down straight across from the elder man.

'It is nothing; do not trouble yourself,' Henry assured him. 'My health has been a tad fickle, as of late. That is all.'

'As has mine,' Falstaff put in. 'Though not through any fault of my own. Your bravo saw to that.'

'Pardon?' Harry asked, momentarily confused. Then he realised Dick must have thought that he, Henry, had hired the man who'd hurt the younger doctor weeks ago. 'Oh, I see. You believe I am somehow responsible for the recent attack upon your person.'

'Ah, we are being frank, then,' observed Falstaff. 'Very well. In that case, I will have you know I do not appreciate your sending that horrid little lover of yours out to do your dirty work.'

'What?!' Henry found himself asking, stupefied by the scenario Dick had suggested.

How utterly ludicrous! he thought. *Lovers?! Of all the far-fetched—*

Then he reflected that the truth, though *he'd* grown used to it, was, in all reality, stranger still.

'I beg your pardon?' he asked Falstaff.

'Don't sound so shocked,' Dick reprimanded him. 'I know all about you two.' He didn't, naturally, but wagered Henry could not know this piffling detail.

'Do you?' the senior physician asked, flabbergasted but also finding the entire situation a bit humorous, even *amusing*.

'Oh, yes,' Dick asserted. 'You and Uncle Harry—excuse me, "the esteemed, late Dr Denman"—are so alike. Both of you taking younger men; both of you trying to protect that old bat, Madge; both of you desiring to sully everything of import in my life, especially my person. And all the while you look so much the saint to the ignorant fools we inappropriately refer to as our "peers". Bloody hypocrites, the both of you.'

'Falstaff, that is the furthest thing from what I've set before myself to do!' Henry exclaimed, hurt, to the charge that all he wished was to make the younger man's life a living misery. *After all,* he thought with pity, bitterness, and just a trace of pleasure, *Dick is doing a fine job of that all on his own.* Aloud, he continued only, 'I came here this evening not to wage war, but to make peace!'

'Afraid you're losing?' shot back Falstaff with a sneer.

'It is no longer a battle,' Harry explained. 'This pointless conflict has diminished both our lives for far too long. We are not exactly young, either of us. We've only so many years left before we go. Why waste those that remain on hateful bickering?'

'Ha. So you *do* admit I've won.'

'Won? Did you even hear me, man? This is no game. There is no war. I withdraw, I make peace, I offer you a friend you may confide in without worry—if only you will let me do these things.'

Ah, thought Dick. *So that's his game. He hopes to lure me into confiding in him, thereby giving away even more of my secrets, so that he may extort me into seeing after that irascible old widow and her overactive ragamuffin, without any fear whatever of me laying bare his epilepsy. Clever old cad. Foolish of him to think I wouldn't see through his tidy little scheme, though.* The situation thus arrayed within his mind, Falstaff took on an air of self-applause, feeling much superior to the hapless elder fellow sitting before him. *Why, it is almost too easy*, he thought, formulating a plan. *Sometimes I outdo even myself.*

'What say you, Dick?' asked Henry, waiting for Falstaff's response to his entreaty. 'Might we make this madness cease?'

Upon the other's answer, Harry felt, hung the fate of both their souls, or at least their dignity.

Falstaff stood up...as did Henry, in response. The latter did not notice that his host had taken off one of his gloves.

'What say I?' Dick echoed, readying his glove in his right hand. Without warning, he snapped it, hard, against the unsuspecting doctor's cheek. 'There!' exclaimed Falstaff at an utterly speechless Henry. 'There is your answer, you damnable dog! And in case you are slow, here it is again!' So saying, he gave a backhand slap to Harry's other cheek, the smack of the glove's leather producing a brief but audible reverberation along the walls and floor of the cramped room. 'Do not speak to me of reconciliation, you traitorous wretch! Your kind are all alike! I'll not be made a fool of ever again, you lying scoundrel!'

With this, he shoved the elder doctor down—an unlikely feat under normal circumstances, given Henry's superior size. So shocked had Falstaff's visitor been by his host's conduct, however, that he'd let himself be pushed to the ground before he'd even realised what was happening. Harry landed on the floor with a resounding thud.

'Is everything alright, sir?' came the muffled voice of Harberson from beyond the door.

'Everything is perfect! Now leave us alone and get back to your duties!' Falstaff growled.

Bertram hurriedly complied, fearing to displease his master further. The sound of his footsteps retreated rapidly down the hall, then fell out of hearing altogether.

'Now, where were we?' Dick asked rhetorically as Harberson made himself scarce. 'Ah, yes,' he said, his face filled with utter contempt, watching a stunned Henry stand shakily back up.

'That was most uncalled for!' accused the elder gent. He'd come here offering the olive branch and had received a cannon blast in return. 'Such audacity is unbefitting even one such as yourself!'

'Don't condescend to me!' Dick hurled back. 'Was it called for, what your bravo did to me?'

Harry sighed. He could see this was going nowhere. Despite his wish that things could have been different, there was simply nothing for it. He spotted his hat and cloak on the rack where Bertram had put them. Fingering his walking stick, he took a couple of steps in their direction but soon found himself waylaid by a rather stubborn Falstaff.

'Where do you fancy you're going?' he asked, blocking the doctor's path with his injured form.

'I am leaving,' informed Henry, attempting to get past the hateful fellow. 'The sooner I depart this place, the better.'

'You're not leaving until *I* say so!' exclaimed Dick, literally and figuratively not budging an inch.

'I beg to differ,' said the elder doctor simply. He slowly but forcibly pushed his way past Falstaff, coming at last to the stand with his hat and cape.

'How dare you?!' spat Falstaff, his jaw jutting out in righteous indignation. 'To mistreat an injured man in his own home!'

'I suppose I am simply returning your peculiar kind of hospitality,' remarked Harry, his back to Dick as he put on his cloak. He grabbed his hat. 'Now, if you will excuse me, I would rather not be here.' So saying, he took hold of the doorknob, giving it a mighty tug as he prepared to exit.

Nothing happened. The door would not budge. Henry cast a look at Dick.

'What's this about?' the hapless houseguest queried, annoyed but also alarmed he couldn't leave.

'As I informed you previously, my dear, dull-witted doctor, you will stay in this room until *I* decide otherwise.'

Henry sighed, exasperated.

'If you have something to say to me, then say it, Richard, and let's have done with it.' For he suspected Falstaff wouldn't let him go until he'd said his piece in all its fullness. Harry estimated this might take a while, and resolved to remain civil during the (no doubt) ensuing tirade. Dick had a lot of problems Henry simply couldn't solve.

Nor can Falstaff himself, for that matter, the elder man of medicine reflected. Still, he did not want to let the poor, vindictive fool drag him down with him, and so Harry made a decided effort to keep calm, remembering at all times that Dick was not well, on a personal level—that the mean, unhappy man could never trust and, so, could never truly love.

Thus steeled against whatever venom Falstaff chose to spew, Henry let Dick harangue him, on and on. When the deluge of bilious insults finally concluded, the elder man simply stood there, silently. In truth, he'd only half-heard all the words Falstaff had hurled his way, preoccupied as he'd been with keeping Dick in a sorrowful, human perspective.

'What do you think of *that*?' his host asked, his tone full of vengeance and satisfaction.

Harry, who had been standing before Falstaff the whole time, at first said nothing. Then, with compassion in his eyes, he clapped a hand on Dick's uninjured shoulder, and told him solemnly, 'I'm sorry for all the troubles you've endured, Richard. Truly sorry. I'd rather they never have happened, but such things are beyond my power. I hope the latter portion of your life is kinder to you than your early years. And God grant you the peace to recognise it.'

Falstaff stood there, stunned, pure bafflement spread out across his face. Then his visage darkened, confusion giving way to smouldering rage.

'DAMN YOU!' he suddenly cried, hurling a punch at Henry before the doctor had any chance to duck out of its way. 'I DON'T NEED YOUR PITY! HOW *DARE* YOU PATRONISE ME?! *CURSE YOU!*' He kicked the elder man savagely in the groin, causing him to collapse to the floor in a whimpering heap. Dick continued to assault him, shouting, 'Bloody hypocrite! Don't make as if you cared—you're all alike! Hiding behind that pretty façade, doing whatever you please to me when no one is looking, pretending there's a scrap of decency in you! I know your tricks! YOU'LL NEVER MAKE A FOOL OF DICK FALSTAFF AGAIN!'

As Harry lay there, being beaten, struggling unsuccessfully to rise, Dick's words came at him from what seemed a great, far distance; the unrelenting pain inflicted on his person rendered all these phrases most surreal. Yet he was cognisant enough to catch their meaning, to protest silently, within his head, against the cruel epithets that stung him more than blows. He was not a hypocrite! He did not *pretend* to be a good man! He was as much himself when he laboured patiently, under the eye of day and sometimes long into the night, to improve the lot of humankind, to save lives in the hospital, to teach a new generation the rigors and complexities of medicine, to help the unfortunate, giving hope to the sick and comfort to the loved ones of those he could not save—he was just as much himself when he performed these admirable endeavours as when he plunged himself into indignity and vice. In all these things, he was himself; he was no pretender! But Falstaff... What good was to be found in that spiteful man? Did he possess any honour, courage, caring? Had he ever shown the least spark of compassion? Was there any redeeming quality whatsoever? The answer, of course, was 'no'. Henry knew it: 'no', 'no', 'no'. That's all Dick was: a great, vast vortex of 'no', of negativity, set to suck down anyone fool enough to draw overly near. The man was a hateful bastard; that was that. There was nothing for it.

Crouched like a leering gargoyle over Harry, Falstaff continued to pummel the doctor's face, his ribs, his abdomen...and other, tenderer portions of man's anatomy. Without warning, Dick felt a tremor run through him, then another, and another, for no apparent reason. As these tremblings sped up in frequency, the younger doctor realised that they were not his own, but emanated, rather, from beneath him. A split second after Falstaff had reached this conclusion, his victim went into a fit of uncontrollable spasming.

Falstaff backed away. He wasn't sure what had come over him. Not that he honestly regretted anything he'd done to Henry, but it simply wasn't good form to strike a guest in one's home. His mind began searching for ways he might stop word of this attack from getting out.

Meanwhile, Harry convulsed helplessly on the floor, apparently caught up in a bout of epilepsy—*quite possibly brought on by my assault*, Dick concluded. His mind was racing now, trying to fashion an excuse that might explain away the bruises on his guest's face, the welts upon his torso, the... Dick realised it was futile. Everyone would find out, would hear of the base savagery of which the esteemed Dr Falstaff, M.D., a pillar of the community, was capable.

'I shall be ruined!' he yelped, knowing there was no way out this time. 'Unless...' A ghastly plan occurred to him. 'A trifle gruesome,' he acknowledged under his breath, 'but it will have to do.' So saying, he took a large knife of oriental make out from its jewelled, decorative display.

The formidable blade unsheathed, he made his way over to his houseguest, who had managed to turn onto his stomach in all his spasming, his cape now covering him over as the last tiny tremors slowly ebbed themselves away.

Dick Falstaff knelt over the dark mass, prepared to burn the rug it lay upon as soon as he had finished this grim business. Harberson, he knew, would help him move the body and tell no one. *Good man, Harberson,* he reflected, *for a servant.*

He raised the knife, ready to plunge it through the cloak and into the cruelly battered flesh beneath.

A flash of black suddenly obscured his vision. Dick struggled, feeling something about his face. *Cloth?* he thought, dropping the ornate dagger in his confusion. He then most unexpectedly found himself shoved against a wall. The impact to his skull sent the dark fabric flying free. He noted, in an unthinking, abstracted way (though not without some surprise), that it was Henry's cape. *Then where*, his mind automatically wondered, *is Docto*—

A gnarled hand laid hold of his throat. Sputtering, Dick struggled just to breathe. He willed his eyes to focus on the visage now before him. He recognised it. It was the bloke from the bordello, Henry's bravo. But wait... Hadn't he and the doctor been the only ones in the room? And hadn't he himself locked the door to ensure that it remained so? Then how—

'Laughable fool,' growled his assailant, staring Falstaff level in the eye, his gaze mad with menace.

Wait a minute, Falstaff thought. Something strange occurred to Dick as he beheld the foul blackguard before him. He looked the fellow over as best he could from his dangerous and uncomfortable position, glancing up and down, from head to toe. He realised what seemed so odd: The man was Falstaff's height. *But he was little more than dwarfish when I first encountered him*, Dick recalled. Then his thoughts were abruptly interrupted as he felt a sea of pain rush out from his most vulnerable of places.

Seeing Dick thus incapacitated, the vengeful villain at once lowered his knee, then hurled the mewling Falstaff to the ground.

'I gave you a chance, you bloody ingrate!' the madman shouted. 'That's one chance more than ever you deserved!'

In a high-pitched, pain-filled voice, a bewildered Falstaff managed:

'What are you talking about, you maniac? All you've done is make my life a living nightmare!'

'No, Dick,' countered his attacker, stalking closer. 'That, you did yourself.' He squatted over the injured man, flipping him onto his back, then pressed his knee solidly into the doctor's chest, his face intruding uncomfortably close to Dick's, dark eyes boring into the depths of his soul. Dick tried to avoid his gaze, shutting his eyes with a wince.

'Look at me, you cowardly little worm!' the fiend commanded, with a hard backhand *whap* to Dick's cheek. He'd be damned if Falstaff was going to get out of this one.

'What do you want from me?!' the latter cried, confused and helpless before his assailant.

'What I want, you cannot give. You're just a miserable, selfish little bastard, a hypocrite who takes and takes and takes! And if anyone sees through you, what then transpires? You do your damnedest to drag him through the mud as well. And should anyone dare try to help you—God forbid!—down he goes, too, into the bloody pit! So, congratulations, Falstaff. You've succeeded. *You win.*' He looked down at his hapless prey. 'Bit of a Pyrrhic victory, wouldn't you say?'

'Who *are* you?' howled Dick out of fear and pure bewilderment.

'I'm Henry, you twit. The man you were just talking with.'

Falstaff looked him over. Had he heard him right? This man was obviously more deranged than he'd imagined.

Perhaps he is a patient of the doctor's, rather than a lover, it belatedly occurred to Dick. Then he noticed something unsettling about this fellow: he was injured. This observation normally would not have been alarming—in fact, if not for the meaning it now signified, Dick would have welcomed it—but Falstaff, ever the physician, marked a chilling familiarity to the madman's welts and bruises. They were in the very spots where he had so savagely laid into Henry not minutes before. There was no way anyone could have duplicated the wounds' placement so precisely.

'Not only that, but I did lock the door,' Dick whispered softly, thinking aloud without being aware of it. 'Which means—'

'Yes,' the rogue cut him off. 'Now you're getting it.'

Dick simply stared at him, the impossible realisation warping Falstaff's face in a fantastic look of horror. Then a hand closed about his throat ere he could scream.

'And by the by,' added Henry, tightening his hold into a death-grip, 'I've *never* had epilepsy.'

CHAPTER TWENTY-SEVEN

A strange man limped along a fog-covered street, swinging his walking stick to and fro as he went. If not for his fear of policemen, he would've whistled a merry tune. As it was, he contented himself with thinking on the deed he'd done tonight. An irrepressible, gleeful smile ran like a nasty gash across his bruised and battered face. His walk, though light-footed, was also a bit stiff, as if his clothes concealed some injury. The garments themselves were overly large, seemingly having been tailored with some other man in mind. He would have made a most unusual sight indeed, had anyone spotted him. As it was, he got to his intended destination unmolested.

'A Mr Harold Edwards to see you, sir,' John was informed by one of his servants, coming into the study. 'Shall I let him in?'

John, who had been reading a pious work of some dryness, looked up with troubled mind.

'"Harold Edwards", did you say?' he asked, concerned.

'Yes, sir. So he claims. Shall I send him off?'

'No,' John said suddenly. 'No, let him in, Carson. Show him to the drawing room and tell him I'll be down to see him presently.'

'Very good, sir.' Carson left to do as his master bade.

John sighed wearily, though not without an undercurrent of anxiety. *What has Henry gone and got himself into this time?* he wondered.

***

The lawyer's mutable friend, meanwhile, had situated himself nicely in the drawing room, lounging upon the sofa, quite at ease. This was how John found him when he came down.

'Ah, good to see you, John,' his guest greeted, pleasantly enough, shifting his feet off the couch as the other man entered.

The attorney, who had been busy closing the door, now turned to face his friend, preparing to ask what was the trouble, but instead simply gave a yelp of surprise upon seeing the latter's condition.

'God's blood, Harry, what happened?!' he exclaimed, referring to the welter of welts and scratches upon the other's face.

'Falstaff,' spoke the visitor, simply enough. He rose up stiffly, favouring his right side.

John worriedly made his way over.

'Is it serious?' he asked, for, in truth, his friend looked like the walking dead, his movement clearly hampered, his face a mess of purple, black, and blue.

'It appears worse than it is,' Henry replied. 'Nothing lethal, though it's rather less than pleasant.'

Having approached closer to inspect the injured man, John noticed a change of some concern to him.

'Henry, are you...taller?' asked the attorney.

'Hm?' responded his guest, glancing about, then down at himself, seemingly comparing his height to John's. Though still shorter than the solicitor, it was by fewer inches than when he'd last paid John a visit in this guise. 'It appears so,' he observed, taking in this new development with a mix of curiosity and pride. 'I seem to be finally up to a more average height.'

'How curious,' said John.

'Not at all.'

'Pardon?'

'It is not at all curious that I've grown. Do you remember the case statement, John?'

'Yes. What of it?'

'I believe I have explained this once already, but I'll go over it again, since you apparently don't recall. I wrote therein about this very phenomenon, theorising it signified the so-called "balance" of my nature. Thus, in the form you choose to term as "normal"—and I, too, when I am in that painful state—I am, as you know, a man of some height and decent build. Whereas, in my current guise, I am much smaller—and, indeed, began as shorter still. But it appears the loathsome Falstaff has given me ample opportunity to "get out", as it were, to exercise this particular facet of my being, inducing, as he has, the change to this more... How shall I put it...? *Uncomplicated* of states. And much more pleasant, incidentally. Thus, the balance has been tipping ever further toward this one. I imagine it shall be even when I reach the height of my "normal", woefully divided self. Still quite a ways to go, in my opinion.' He looked at John. 'Does that clear things up for you?'

'I should say so, though it is worrisome,' the lawyer acknowledged.

'Whatever makes you say that, friend? Should you not be happy for me? I have found a cure for my affliction.'

'Truly?' asked John, not having expected this. 'Do you mean to say you've found a way to turn back to your usual self without trouble?'

This would be a blessing and relief to the attorney, who, despite his encouraging words to the doctor, had feared Henry would never find a cure.

'No, I mean to say that you are looking at the remedy as we speak.'

John's face filled with pity and consternation.

'You cannot be serious,' he pronounced.

'I am deadly serious, my old friend. Have you any idea what it is like being tortured by one's conscience all the time, a slave to prudish morality and the ridiculous demands of propriety, never slipping their yoke but for a few glorious instants, only to have the whole weight of one's shortcomings and iniquities come crashing down upon the soul, condemning every act or thought that makes one feel *alive*? And do you know what it is like to be constantly surrounded by the hypocrites so wrongly referred to as "peers"... Do you know how awful it is to have condemned oneself, and yet to see these hateful, double-dealing frauds walking about, not a care in the world, without a lick of conscience to their supposedly "honourable" names? They do whatever they please without any suffering, with no remorse, uncaring that the morals they so staunchly uphold by day and so freely violate at night have formed themselves into a noose about the neck of one half-decent fellow—someone who actually gave a damn!—that he then suffers, thanks to their fine lies. And when, finally, this fellow finds release, risks death and his soul on the off-chance his torment will cease—when this miraculous event occurs, what then transpires? The very folk who gave rise to his malady, who are the blackest hypocrites of all—these hunt the fellow down, calling him "blackguard", "villain", "fiend", and worse... Even this gentleman's friend has a hatred of him, knowing not who it is or what he's endured.

'And then, at last, when all cards are on the table and the friend can see the happy truth before him, what does he say? He labels it an anomaly, a malady, a disease to be cured. The true sickness is not the bruised and battered form you see before you, John. It lies within your poor friend's heart, a despair born of restriction and too-high moral standards, of hatred of oneself for being only human, of taking to heart the guidelines one is handed down, while everyone else ignores them at their pleasure.' He looked at his friend and confidant. 'If the balance tips, it tips, John. I care not.' Reflecting a moment, he added, 'Save for the attentions of the law.'

'You mean "consequences",' the attorney clarified.

'If that is how you wish to word it. Yes.'

John sighed. This was such a damnably complicated situation...

'Well, if nothing else, stay clear of that Dick Falstaff,' the lawyer advised his friend.

'That will not be a problem,' returned Henry with a knowing smile.

John didn't like the look of it. 'What do you mean?'

'Only that he shall no longer trouble me.' He took off his cape, which had heretofore covered him over. The inside was stained through and through with blood. So were his clothes.

'Henry!' John exclaimed. 'What have you done?!'

'Rid the world of a damnable, arrogant bastard.' He saw John's look of alarm. 'And defended myself,' he added, pointing out his injuries. 'You should know: that bloody bugger started it.'

'But what on earth were you even doing in his vicinity? And to kill him?! You could have simply avoided any truck with the man; you and I are both of us aware how he sets you off. Surely you knew—'

'Of course I knew,' interjected John's murderous friend. 'But, like an utter fool, I'd tried to find the good in him, tried to actually sympathise with that spiteful mongrel's plight! Of all things, I thought I could "fix" him, make him come round by making peace. I thought he was like unto me. But I was wrong. He'd have none of it. So,' he reflected, 'I "fixed" him in a different way. For good.'

John said nothing, trying to come to grips with the fact that his dear old friend Harry, whom he'd known for decade upon decade, seen at pleasant dinner parties, had many a stimulating conversation with—Henry, who laboured for the greater good, who sincerely endeavoured to ease the suffering of many (and often succeeded), who lectured all his students on the miraculous phenomenon of life and how the human body contained it—that this same fellow had just savagely ended another man's existence; more than that, stood here, seemingly self-satisfied, drenched in the poor fool's blood.

John shook his head. 'Harry,' he said, shaken and with utmost seriousness of tone, unthinkingly using the more informal version of his friend's name in an attempt to get through to him, 'this is terrible. The man is dead. I know Falstaff is—was—an unpleasant fellow, but this...' He sighed, looking at his unrepentant chum. 'This is a terrible mess, you know.'

'Don't worry; it appears a suicide.'

'Come again?' John asked, confused. Then a sickening feeling of shock and abhorrence began to sink through the lawyer's being as it dawned on him what Henry might've done. He feared what his friend would say next, prayed it wasn't what his mind was just on the verge of realising. Unfortunately, his hunch (as was so often the case) proved right.

'It looks as if Falstaff committed the act of self-slaughter,' explained Henry. 'Apparently, he stabbed himself in the throat. Quite thoroughly. He hit both the carotid artery and the jugular vein. Bled to death in minutes. Of course, with his knowledge of anatomy, it's patent that he must have meant to do this.' He looked up toward the ceiling, contemplating the hypothetical scenario. 'He must have been most weary of this life, one would surmise.'

'*Henry.*' John closed his eyes. 'Cease. Speaking.' A wave of anger threatened to take him over—a rare occurrence for the typically unflappable attorney.

Harry was silent, seeming for a moment both quizzical and hurt. He seated himself quietly on a chair, looking up at John.

The wave passed. So did the doctor's quasi-vulnerable expression.

Taking a breath to calm himself (which he then let out as a rather heavy sigh), John regained his composure and sat upon the drawing-room sofa. He stared into Henry's eyes (though they now looked quite different from the genial, pleasant green hue he was used to), searching for any scrap of the man he thought he knew.

He found it, but it wasn't at all the part he had been looking for. What he saw in the other's gaze was a mix of three distinct expressions he'd till now seen only separately in Henry, on some few occasions in times past. One, the most frequent, had been in evidence whenever the doctor had whispered critical asides to John at parties, after some self-important person or other had walked by them. The second was a wariness, a sort of subdued, panicked cunning, witnessed when Henry spotted any person heading toward him whom he'd rather have avoided, as if the doctor were weighing means of escape. (As these folk tended to be the unpleasant, gossiping, or just plain boring sort, John had usually agreed with his friend on this matter.) But the last element was a spirit of arrogance, combined with hatred—or was it hate-filled rage?—a disgust, an utter contempt, that knew no reasoning, no bounds. Excepting a few forgivable instances in Henry's youth, John had seen this expression on his friend's face only once (prior to his present ordeal, at least), when a student had made a passing, unkind comment about the doctor's then-recently deceased father. John could have sworn, at that time, that Harry'd well intended to leap across the demonstration table and throttle the lad, so black a look had gathered on his countenance. The usually magnanimous professor had shortly thereafter recovered himself, turning his back on the over-rude young pupil, bidding him, with curt politeness, to take his leave post haste.

Before his experiments, these three emotions, normally subdued, had merely lent a faintly slyish cast to his kind eyes; indeed, this still held true when the doctor wore his typical form. Yet his current physical guise magnified them all. Not only that, but there seemed to be nothing else.

So, yes, John concluded, it was Henry, but counted it unfortunate. This wasn't a part of his old friend he'd ever have liked to know.

'Think of your mother,' John said, simply enough. An idea had occurred to him.

'Excuse me?'

'Think of your mother, Harry. Think of what you went through when she passed away. Think of all you lost when she was taken from you. Remember when they put her in the ground, and you knew you would never lay eyes upon her face again, the woman you admired all your boyhood. Think of the day, the very moment, when you lost her for good.' For John knew this had affected Henry deeply. 'Now think on this,' he added. 'The sorrowful jaws of death have now snatched Falstaff away, too.' He looked his friend solemnly in the eye as he dropped the final words, like so many weighty millstones: *'By your hand.'*

'That bastard was *nothing* like my mother,' Harry spat, trembling with anger. He glowered at his friend as if sensing the ruse. 'That was rather low of you, John.'

I am trying to help you, thought the lawyer silently, with inner adamance, *if you will only stop hating long enough to listen.* Outwardly, he said simply, 'I did not intend it to be. It was merely something which occurred to me, and to which I gave voice. Perhaps I should not have. But tell me, how am I to view Falstaff's demise, then? What else could I possibly have thought? Death is harsh, no matter where it happens, or to whom.'

'I do not think it was any mere passing thought you chose to voice, but very well, let us forget that for the moment. I shall answer your question.' He drew himself up, looking John square in the eye. 'What could you have thought, you ask? It is really quite straightforward: Rather than condemning me, casting the accusatory glare, bringing up a subject which I even now find painful—and of this fact, I *know* you are aware, so don't bother saying differently—rather than choosing to take such childish actions and hurl such churlish words, upon hearing of the loathsome blighter's death, you could simply have congratulated me.'

'Congratulated you?' John echoed incredulously, a hint of worry in his tone.

'Whatever for?' He wasn't entirely sure he wanted to know, but reasoned that Henry's answer might enable him to figure out where his friend was coming from and, therefore, how his mental state might best be affected... and, potentially, altered for the better.

'Why, for ending the miserable lout's life, of course,' came the reply. 'For finally getting past all those moronic social barriers of protocol and simply strangling the life out of him. Well, almost; the dagger did the final deed—the selfsame instrument with which he attempted to slay me, I might put in. For actually thinking enough of myself to give the bugger what for, when he so very clearly deserved it. For making him rue the day he *ever* decided to get on my bad side. Such things are not without consequence, you know.' He looked pointedly at his host before continuing. 'I served him back tenfold, before it was done; I committed upon his person the very crime of which he'd accused me, then snuffed out his hateful existence with much pleasure. At last, that dog got what was long in coming to him. And *by my hand*, no less.' A sly, malefic smile spread across his lips as he waited for John's reaction to these revelations.

The lawyer said nothing at first, wondering if Henry had *any* limits when he was in this way, any redeeming qualities, anything to give him personal worth at all. He concluded that the only meaningful characteristic of Harry's right now was that he might yet revert to his typical state, once more become the friend John thought he knew. He would never be able to look at the man the same way again, though, knowing what existed within him.

Privately, he wondered if a similar monster mightn't reside inside himself as well. He shuddered inwardly.

Then, something else happened: he felt sorry for his friend, despite—or perhaps because of—the latter's disagreeable state. He could not really blame him, though a part of him wanted to. But this, he knew, was the worst part, and he resolved not to give in to it. Harry's was a lamentable case altogether— extraordinary, baffling, just plain *strange*— but lamentable for all that. And the bottom line was John could not, in good conscience, blame his friend if he knew that he, the esteemed attorney, might, somewhere, in the darkness of his being, be like unto the foul creature before him. To do so would've been the height of hypocrisy, and though the lawyer tolerated his share (and more) of double-dealers, he still harboured no wish to fall among them.

'I do not care,' said John simply. 'Whatever you have done, I shall not abandon you. You are human, as are we all. I will not condemn you. Such things are beyond me, or I beyond them.' He looked the blood-drenched doctor over. 'Come,' he pronounced, standing up, 'we had better see about those clothes. They are not exactly inconspicuous.' After all, it wouldn't do to have anyone find the unfortunate fellow in this state, much less these incriminating garments. John felt he must attempt to stem the damage. He owed a friend no less, knowing Henry would have done the same and more for him had their positions somehow been reversed.

So thinking, the lawyer took a step toward his frightful guest, intending to take the blood-soaked garb and throw it in the fireplace, thus destroying any evidence that the doctor was ever involved in this night's tragedy.

Yet, before John had moved forward half a foot, he saw a look, a change in Harry's eye, followed thereupon by violent tremblings, the doctor's pupils dilating as he fell upon the floor, thrashing about. He seemed to swell.

Two thoughts entered the lawyer's mind, near-simultaneously: He felt untold relief, nigh ecstasy, at witnessing this change for his friend's good, and it occurred to him, *That old rug shall be ruined*, as he watched the other man spasm, in his bloody clothes, upon the drawing-room floor.

Gasping, shaking, Henry came to himself, weak and trembling from the strain upon his person. He looked up to his steadfast friend from the low place where he now lay, not even able to sit up as of yet.

'I was testing you, John,' he half-managed to say, through wobbly lips. A line of drool spilled down onto the rug. 'God forgive me, I was testing you.' Ashamed, he could no longer meet John's gaze.

The attorney raised his eyebrows. Testing him? What—?

Of course, he realised suddenly, inside his incredulous mind. In a flash, it all made sense. *The last time I spoke to Harry in that state, it was my dedication, my professed but, at the time, only yet philosophical loyalty, which brought him round unto his normal self. It appears that, this time, he aimed to ascertain that the depth of our friendship was not merely theoretical—that I had not been lying, that I would be true to my word and stick by him.*

'Apparently, I've passed,' the lawyer answered (rather wryly, given the circumstances), his nonchalant tone layered atop a very real relief.

On hands and knees, and heaving for each breath, the doctor hung his head in shame, glancing upon the ruined and bloodstained rug. Thoughts filled his head: the memory of Falstaff's dying, the gross indecencies that the poor man had suffered before the end, the surge of power and glee Henry'd known as he'd humiliated, then destroyed, the fellow who'd provoked him to this madness. Yet he knew it was himself he had to blame; his conscience, back now from its buried prison, burst forth to spring at him, all teeth and claws, shredding him with sharp stings of contrition and remorse. He could not move from where he found himself, tormented by his vicious recollections, regret and guilt so strong they caused him almost physical pain, hampered his breathing...

He began to sob, collapsed upon the floor in bloodstained cloak, the weight of everything—Falstaff's death, his foul experiments, the mistakes of his youth, the pointlessness and folly of his entire existence—all this ran him through, punched him to the gut, and, in time, robbed him of the very strength to weep. He lay there, numb and sorrowful, at a loss for knowing how to live, how to go on, or whether he should, but uncertain how to die. To take any action at this point was quite beyond him. Everything was fruitless. He wasn't sure if he even knew how to feel, so great was the depth of despair that swept him under. He ached, both metaphorically and physically. He could still feel his tears' wet residue upon his cheeks, though their springs ran dry.

He took a deep breath, then let it out. He rose into a kneel, not really thinking about it, but aware of it all the same. Everything seemed...distant. Was he really in this room? Was he really the man he thought he was (whatever that meant)? Was that really John there, beholding him with a look of concern and confusion, perplexed by the show of emotion, and weighing which way he ought to respond? Henry felt the urge to laugh at himself, his predicament, his life (or what passed for it); it would have been a piteous, rueful laugh, a sound condemning all he'd known as false—a funny lie, a painful truth. But he had not even the energy for that. He looked down at the floor, bloodstains tainting the carpet on which he found himself. His eyes wandered over them unthinkingly, charting their blackish-red traceries, a study in beauty and gore.

'Harry,' John said, bending down, half-kneeling, till he came to his friend's level. 'Harry. Can you hear me?' He waved a hand in front of Henry's face, the worry growing. 'Are you here?'

Henry drew in a breath as the lawyer (mercifully) broke in upon his melancholic fugue, shattering it to pieces with his presence, remnants of the reverie shaken swiftly off as the physician came back to himself—to the real world of his current situation. His eyes came into focus, fixing upon his friend, his saviour, then upon his own dark, bloodied garments.

'You're right, John,' he said, a little abruptly, as the thought came back to him. 'We should burn these. No good can come of my being inside them.' Within the doctor's heart, there formed a gratitude so deep it could not be expressed in any words. He was alive. He was safe. He was repentant. He was himself.

He had been saved. Again.

And then regret came sweeping in afresh.

'I have killed the man, John,' he said, the gravity of the deed catching up with him as what he'd done sank in. He could hardly believe it, this horrible act; the whole night seemed some sort of surreal nightmare. 'I set out with good intentions,' he remarked, more to himself than the solicitor, as he recalled the fine and optimistic spirit in which he'd left his home that evening, on a mission to prove mercy and compassion could win out. 'I meant to show him kindness, John—for, Lord knows, the fellow needed it. Yet instead...' He could not bring himself to finish as scenes of Dick's last unhappy hour on Earth emblazoned themselves across Harry's mind-field, the sigil of his iniquities searing his very soul, branding his tender heart with a bleeding, blistering, white-hot penitence. His eyes welled up; piteous tears overflowed their natural levies as he turned to look up toward his friend, his witness, his confidant. His heart felt like to burst.

'I didn't mean for it to happen!' he exclaimed, remorse and sadness plain upon his face. 'He didn't deserve—no one deserves... Oh, he was a cad, John, a fraud and a liar, but...even *he* didn't warrant what—what I... did...'

Henry sat then, forehead in palm, in a state of dismay, heartache, sickness, and grief—for Falstaff, for himself, for life's cruel tricks. Did God enjoy this, he wondered—seeing fate and irony hand-in-hand, and woe betide the pitiful fools who thought they could make anything the better—did the Lord and Saviour laugh to see the looks upon their faces, treasuring each bitter, heart-wrenched tear?

But such thoughts only added to his guilt and building lowness. To let himself continue down this course would mean to go down with it, to its murky, gloom-black, unforgiving end. He could not afford that. He knew it, and John knew it. The attorney hadn't done much else but listen, especially during his friend's wretched, tearful torrent of emotion, but he knew enough to recognise the danger in letting Henry sit and brood on his pain-filled feelings. He removed the doctor's blood-spattered cape before the latter had any chance for further lamentation.

Surprised out of his ponderings, Harry asked, 'Whatever are you—?' then stopped as John threw the fine accoutrement into the waiting flames.

'I am disposing of the evidence,' the lawyer explained, more in response to the look on his friend's face than to his aborted earlier half-query. He glanced Henry over, noting in particular the starched, white dress shirt with its lacework of dried crimson. Somehow, it seemed, the trousers had escaped the brunt of the blood-spray, but, John reasoned, better safe than sorry. '*All* the evidence,' he clarified.

Harry looked from the fire to his raiments. He understood.

Everything burned quite well, despite the bloodstains.

CHAPTER TWENTY-EIGHT

A bloodstained floor was all that remained when the inspectors finished examining the ghoulish scene at the home of the late Dr Richard Falstaff. The knife had been taken away for evidence, the remaining household staff thoroughly questioned, and the bodies long since hauled away to the morgue.

Bod*ies*. A maidservant of Falstaff's had found two of them when she'd walked through the drawing room's unlocked door. Her screams had alerted the rest of the servants in the house...all but one.

They found him lying next to what remained of the doctor, his hand resting upon the dagger that had ended both their lives. This lay plunged deep into the poor fellow's chest, having found its target and accomplished its sad deed. The sawbones conducting the autopsy declared it self-inflicted.

His heart pierced and broken, Bert Harberson had followed his dear master to the grave.

CHAPTER TWENTY-NINE

The city's papers were soon filled with the strange and tragic tale of this ghastly murder-suicide. Wealthy Londoners dozed uneasily within their warm and comfortable beds; even those whose domestics had served faithfully for decades upon end now found themselves (often with less-than-conscious intent) casting a baleful eye of suspicion where not the slightest hint of doubt had ever crept in before. After all, if the lowly, unobtrusive manservant of Falstaff's could (many assumed) commit so frightfully foul a deed upon so eminent a member of the vaunted upper crust...why, no man, prince or pauper, could sleep safe.

It thus hit home with a great many of society's most influential, well-off members that their pretty illusions of pampered, special security were, in fact, nothing more than pleasant, foolish fictions—mirages much too dangerous to idly accept. Having thus been robbed of their accustomed sense of highborn invulnerability, of the expected safety their entitled privilege provided, they set to reassure themselves that they were far beyond the reach of such deadly misfortune, that they would never share poor Falstaff's fate. To this end, they did what they did best, putting forth another neat, fine lie. It was concocted from the known facts of the case, but soon gave way to unabashed, guilt-placing speculation, blaming Dick for his own demise (though not at all in the manner this had actually occurred). Rumours of a wild, pernicious nature made the rounds not long after Doctor Falstaff's death. No one would admit to starting these, of course, but everyone knew their contents all the same. The rough outline of suspicion ran something like this: Dick and his (assumedly) murderous manservant, Harberson, had been on rather closer terms than proper. At some point in their dubious relationship, a time had come when something had gone awry. A quarrel had then ensued, rife (no doubt) with jealousies and hurtful, piercing words. During the impassioned argument, Bertram, in a pique of heart-stung rage, had grabbed the nearby, gold-sheathed, deadly knife and ended his poor master's sorry life. This red deed, however, having been committed in the unthinking insanity of passion, hadn't been what Harberson had wanted at all. Upon realisation of the terrible thing he had done, the wretched Bert, with guilt-wracked, broken heart, had then enacted his own punishment. Lying by his now-dead master's side, he'd plunged the unhappy dagger deep between his own ribs, leaving his heart's blood to spill out across the floor, mingling with that of the man he had so dearly, *closely* served till death.

It thus came about that Falstaff suffered scandal at his own grim funeral, at the hands (or wagging tongues) of those high folk he'd most sought to impress. At his very burial, as he was lowered down into the clammy, oversaturated ground, the rain falling in tear-like drops upon the sombre coffin—even at this sad affair, the seeming well-wishers did naught but gossip in hushed tones, their whispers soiling any scrap of honour he had left. All took quiet enjoyment in defiling this man's name, unthinking what their unpitying amusement cost their souls... All but one. This man did not see fit to flagellate poor Falstaff further, ignoring the shameful, tawdry rumours of the rest. He was, in truth, the last chap (besides Cedric) whom one would've expected to turn up here to pay the late physician an earnest adieu.

Yes, Henry was in attendance. He'd felt he could not do otherwise. He had come to pay his last, regret-filled respects to a poor soul he'd more than failed to save. He also thought it would prove sobering to his own, ill-seated conscience, to impress indelibly upon his mind and heart that this, *this*, was the price of his wrongdoings; this, the lethal product of his own loss of control. This morbid, stupid tragedy, where one life more was lost, was what his brief descension into foolish spite had cost. And it would happen again, he reminded himself fiercely, were he not ever-vigilant.

The thought jolted its way through him and he shivered as his blood ran cold.

No, he resolved inside himself, *I will not, shall not, and want not allow such pointless, evil, damned waste of life to ever transpire by my hand again! God forgive me (if indeed such grace is possible) for all the wretched horrors I have wrought! If I could but take them back—undo the sordid sorrows I have sown!—but it is futile; who in this vale of tears can turn back time?* Here he turned his gaze once more upon the yawning, dampened soil where Falstaff lay, the mourning skies and dripping grass the only source of tears for this passed man. *Oh, God, they have laid him in the earth,* Harry observed, still to himself. With horrid realisation, *He is really, truly dead,* the heartless fact sank in. *That's it. That's all. That's all.*

The gravediggers began to shovel dirt onto the lid of what would now be Falstaff's final home.

He's gone, the guilt-drenched doctor thought. *Soon he will be buried deep, sealed up forever in that cold, black tomb—on my account!*

Henry could stand to see this sight no longer, and left the grounds as soon as he was able to get free from the mob of gossiping pretenders at the gravesite.

Going back inside the damp-stoned church (now all but deserted, it appeared), he leaned against a side, nave wall, the blackness of his raiments a dark pool against cool stone of mottled grey. Though he still found no respite from his painful, guilt-filled thoughts, which even now churned mercilessly through his weary mind, the church's chill interior did soothe his nerves somewhat, relieving him from the prim strain of being in the well-bred crowd outside. Here, at least, within this silent sanctuary, he could just *be*, alone. He could let all true expressions cross his face as he saw fit, swept up in his deep, castigating thoughts, without fear or worry as to how he should appear. There was no one to see him. Here, at last, the troubled sinner found a shade of peace in solitude, in welcome and unbroken privacy.

That is, until a black-clad priest showed up most unexpectedly beside him. Henry nearly jumped out his own throat in his surprise (and unintentional panic), looking very much like a large, songbird-eating feline with a feather clinging to its lip. (Never mind if the cat *did* feel bad about killing the poor thing...)

Such an alarmed reaction was, of course, highly irrational: the minister did not, *could not* know anything regarding Harry's role in making for the funeral outside. The doctor, after all, was now his usual self—had been ever since his talk with John. He had not a wisp of his foul other form about him...save, perhaps, for his brief fear and panic (even if these did give way to guilt). Sheepishness surpassed these two immediately thereon, as Henry recognised his fear-induced reaction for the false alarm it was.

The approaching churchman, though, mistook the look for hard grief, and tried his best to reassure this lost lamb of God's flock.

'I know whereon you think,' said he, assuming the physician a dear friend of the deceased.

Harry started without meaning to at these unanticipated words, managing a simple, 'Oh! Oh. Do you?' in reply—quite neutrally, he thought, given his fresh shock at this unexpected, bold assertion.

'Oh, yes,' intoned the well-intentioned priest, taking the high break in Henry's voice as one more sign of a distraught mourner's sorrow.

The doctor was not certain what to say—nor what to think.

The man of God found this hesitance a further proof of this poor soul's distress.

'He is in another place now,' soothed the shepherd, solemnly, referring to Dick. 'The best that we can do for him is pray.' At this, he gestured, open-palmed, toward one of the pews, indicating that this guest in God's house should fill a seat.

Harry, feeling trapped, could do naught but comply. He had come here for solace, not a sermon, but there was rather little to be done. He did not wish to appear insincere, arouse suspicion, or offend this nosey minister—who, he could tell, was really not a bad sort; his intentions were good.

'I shall pray with you,' pronounced the priest, taking his place just to Henry's left, at the end of the pew.

'That's very good of you,' the tall doctor replied, a bit startled. Yet he wished this well-meaning man would simply go away and leave him to his own process of grief, to sorrows which he had to plumb himself.

The chap was youngish, for a churchman—in his early thirties at most—with blue-green eyes, a bulbous nose, and blondish hair cut short. He looked youthful even for his years, never having quite outgrown his boyhood baby-fat.

'The Lord is full of mercy,' he began, 'slow to anger, quick to forgive.'

Though the man of God had shut his eyes when he'd first clasped his hands, and faced straight forward, and though he could not know the tragic evil Henry'd done—despite these things, the doctor felt this churchman's words were somehow meant for *him*.

'God knows the heart of every man,' the clergyman continued. 'He is with us through the gauntlet of our lives in this poor world, until that final day of glorious reunion with Our Lord. O God, we implore Thee to look after Richard Falstaff, and grant him peace in Thy heav'nly abode. In Thine infinite mercy, forgive the poor sinners in Thy midst. Grant us strength and guidance in these grim and trying times. Thy will be done. Amen.'

He opened his eyes to find the dark lost lamb beside him weeping soundlessly, lids squeezed shut and hands clasped so tightly in prayer that they were white unto the very knuckle. The mourner seemed only by a great effort of will to be controlling the momentary shudders which now and then passed, quake-like, through all his stiffened corpus. The minister (who, though relatively young, had still seen funerals enough to judge reactions) found surprise at this. It was unusual for a gentleman to show so much painful, heartfelt emotion. Why, the fellow seemed barely able to retain control of himself.

Henry had been struck to his core by what the man of God had said to him. He regretted all he'd done, he would sincerely pray for the soul of his unhappy victim, but more than this, the sermon had hit home in further truth: these *were* grim and trying times, the kind that tested a man's faith in God, in himself, in goodness, in a reason for it all—this type of situation tested all these things to the breaking point. This was the moment when poor, crushed souls lost hope, to fall forever into the pit of despair.

Though the lesson-giver probably had no idea he did so, God (Harry felt) was somehow working through him nonetheless. Here was a promise of forgiveness, guidance in the face of sorrowful confusion, hope to beat back utter misery. There was meaning, wasn't there? Surely, the Lord had a purpose, even for him. Otherwise, why was he even still here? Yet here he was, and had been handed a message of forgiveness, from out the lips of a kind, young priest who likely had no idea what weighty import his pious prayer held for this lone mourner. The doctor wept at the profundity of grace, of God's deep Love.

The shepherd had not anticipated his words of mere comfort would provoke such a powerful display of outward emotion, (barely) contained though it was. Men of this fellow's class did not deem it proper to let loose such flows of tears ('stiff upper lip' and all that), even at a dear friend's funeral. Mourning was a private matter, done far away from public eyes; only women wept before the masses. The minister surmised that the shaking man before him (who was only just suppressing powerful sobs) had been to the poor, murdered Dr Falstaff...well, something rather more than a close friend.

Henry felt a hand upon his shoulder. This took a moment to register, pulling him hazily out of his penitent, indescribably grateful, and humbling epiphany. His eyes focused just before the churchman spoke.

'I am truly sorry for your loss,' proclaimed the solemn worker of God's will.

Harry had the urge to thank the man, to say to him, *'Your words have affected me greatly; I cannot describe to you how very much they mean'*, to tell him not to trouble himself on his account. But as he was internally formulating the particular phrasing of this grateful declaration, the man of God continued:

'Loved ones can never be replaced, Lord knows. Yet perhaps,' he conjectured, pressing a slim slip of paper into Henry's palm, 'you may find some solace in this place.' With that and a quick, pious nod, the priest departed.

The doctor was momentarily confused, thinking the young man had perhaps meant the church by 'this place', but this hypothesis soon disintegrated. Left alone to consider the stiff paper he now held, Harry unfolded it, only to find it a most unusual advertisement, done up quite nicely, on the finest stock. It appeared, by the look of it, to be a private invitation of some type, though the first line bore no form of address save 'Dear Sir'. The signature, he discovered, was no name, but simply an address. Henry, with much consternation and just a hint of racing, curious wonder, found himself cordially invited, by way of the (doubtless) well-meaning young minister, to a little-known, apparently upscale establishment (which, as the letter put it, catered to only a 'select clientele')...in London's lurid, infamous East End.

All this took a moment to sink in. Then came the sudden realisation, like a gong to consciousness, of the awful implications this foul invitation had—given to him, as it had been, by a sanctioned (and seeming) 'man of God'.

The depth of the hypocrisy! he thought, blasted by such knowledge, swimming in a sea of fresh resentment tempered by relief. On the one hand, it was, in some small, unadmitted way, a comfort to rediscover he was not alone in sinning, that even the high holy man had his faults. On the other, the doctor was morbidly appalled. *Is no one pure?*

he thought. *Is nothing sacrosanct? Is there not one person on the whole Earth who means all that he says, who appears good and is so, ardently?* For even the priest was not what he'd presumed. It made Harry wonder, *Did he mean one word of what he said? Or was it simply a quaint act he performs well each day? And what does that mean for the words I thought from God? Perhaps it was foolish of me... Am I only a drowning man, grasping at rotten straws...?* And what faith he had left wavered in the wake of this unpleasant revelation.

He was sick of all the falsity—in which he played his part, granted, but he wouldn't have preferred such things that way. The truth was, he did not know just how he would've been, had he not been born into his social stratum, had he not been hampered or (in truth) confined, bound a slave to all the ways a *gentleman* behaved, imprisoned by the pink of the proprieties. Not that it was always bad—in fact, he rather enjoyed being proper, at times; it gave him a genial feeling of respectability and allowed him, in formalities, to express some of the goodwill that he most sincerely felt. He found a joy in courtesy, in kindnesses repaid. It was only that he also had to suffer fools he hated, to respect them in society when they bored him unto tears, to be polite and give a smile to hidebound ignoramuses—it was only this, which proved false courtesy. Otherwise, he really was a rather decent fellow, normally...

This smooth-faced, suave conformity and a buried, merry tendency toward epicurean fun—which he by turns enjoyed and felt ashamed of, and which he had indulged a little less than quietly in youth, then hidden away from all judging, respectable eyes—these were the blackest of the doctor's falsities and sins. Or, rather, they had been. Now, of course, he counted a multitude more, and these graver in character by several orders of magnitude. So high had been his impossible aspirations, so deep, morbid, and abiding his sense of shame at the almost-harmless pleasures he'd sought to hide, that things had fallen out the way they had, leading up to this very moment of self-reflection. And thus it came about that the furtive, guilt-drenched doctor now found himself, twice a murderer, sitting quietly in a dreary Anglican church, an invite to an East End den of vice in his hand, while Falstaff's funeral finished up outside.

Sorrowfully, Henry stood to take his leave, pocketing the folded paper as he did so. Not that he ever intended to visit the address—Heaven forbid! No, he had grown quite sick of sinning, but felt it inappropriate to simply leave the foul letter lying, unabashed, in the chapel's very nave, where Lord-knew-who might chance to pick it up.

Departing the hypocrisy-laden 'house of God', Harry spied the throng that had ringed Falstaff's gravesite beginning to break up, a great, disorderly wave of the finest pitch-black raiments, topped by dark umbrellas drenched in rain. The funeral had ended. Not one among the 'mourners' deigned to give a backward glance to where the former doctor's body lay, fully buried now, cold and, at the last, alone, the one soul who had ever cared to love him flown away, its vacant tabernacle now interred some miles distant, as Bertram rotted in a poor man's plot. Not one tear was shed for Dick at the site of his own grave. The proper mob wended its way away from this grey place, the thoughts of its component persons moving on to other things than this—what would be had for supper, how lovely it should be to come in out of the chill, whether one ought to run by the bank or not on his way home, and many other trifling, mundane concerns. Falstaff lay in the ground silently, already all but forgotten, as the tromping feet of London's best shook off his memory like dust.

The only man alive who cared a whit observed it all from where he stood, still and soundless, peering through the cemetery's sturdy, wrought-iron fence, as the faceless kine trudged toward him through the mud, still gossiping to make themselves feel grand—at a dead man's expense.

Henry could bear to see no more of it. Sad and sickened, he simply turned...and walked away.

CHAPTER THIRTY: EPILOGUE

What was left of Dr Denman's fortune was finally restored to Madge and Ginny after the discovery of the late doctor's will. It was found by a corpse-dresser during the preparation of the equally late Dr Falstaff's body for its funeral. In stripping the bloodied clothes off the dead man (so that he might be buried in his finest suit), a folded, yellowed, newly-bloodstained piece of parchment fell out of an inner pocket of Falstaff's waistcoat—the one he had worn when murdered. Upon closer inspection, this document, still somehow legible, revealed itself to be the aforementioned will. Dick had kept this 'trophy' on his person ever since the vase in which he'd previously stowed it had been smashed to pieces during one of Harry's 'fits'.

These episodes still concerned Dr Henry Jekyll, despite the ostensible good that had come of Falstaff's death. He lived in dread anxiety of the day his malady might again lay hold of him—as it indeed did. But that is a tale for another time...

Author Profile

A. A. Sekhon is the author of the *Passing Normal* series: *Assumptions*, its forthcoming sequels, and its eventual prequel. Sekhon strives to bring the past to life with both compassion and unflinching realism, whether in these works of fiction or teaching at university.

Publisher Information

Rowanvale Books provides publishing services to independent authors, writers and poets all over the globe. We deliver a personal, honest and efficient service that allows authors to see their work published, while remaining in control of the process and retaining their creativity. By making publishing services available to authors in a cost-effective and ethical way, we at Rowanvale Books hope to ensure that the local, national and international community benefits from a steady stream of good quality literature.

For more information about us, our authors or our publications, please get in touch.

www.rowanvalebooks.com
info@rowanvalebooks.com

Paris-Rhone	1947-1950	France
Pasquil-Rhone	1947-1950	France
Peka	1924	Germany
Perfecta	1899-1903	Italy
Rapid	1899-1900	Switzerland
Revolution	1970	GB
Richard	1900s	France
Rinspeed UFO	1983	Switzerland
Rogers Rascal	1980	Canada
R W Kit Cars	1980	GB
RWN	1928-1929	Germany
Samca Atomo	1947-1951	Italy
Sanchis	1906-1912	France
Seetsu	1906-1907	GB
SGS	1983	Switzerland
Shell Valley Apolo	1980s	USA
Shelter	1954-1958	Netherlands
SMZ	1956	USA
Stevens and Croft	1933	GB
Succes	1952	Belgium
Sui Tong Rickshaw	1960-1980	Taiwan
Sui Tong Cub	1982-1983	Taiwan
Sunrise	1980	USA
Sycar	1915	GB
SZL	1956-1969	USSR
Tamag	1933	Germany
Thrift-T	1955	USA
Titan	1911	GB
Toboggan	1905-1906	GB
Torpelle	1914	France
Tri-Vator	1980	USA
TST	1922	GB
Tyseley-Unicar	1911	GB
Velomobile	1905-1907	Germany
VH	1961	Spain
Wendaz	1931	Germany
Wesnigk	1920-1923	Germany
Zetgelette	1923	Germany

The Pennington Autocar 1897.
Advertised as the fastest machine in the world in a 'motor car run' from Coventry to a Birmingham pub, the Swan at Yardley.
A rather extraordinary publicity photo of this early '3-wheeler'. *(author's collection)*